Farewell to Russia

Other Voices of Italy

Editors: Eilis Kierans, Alessandro Vettori, and Sandra Waters

This series presents texts in a variety of genres originally written in Italian. Much like the symbiotic relationship between the wolf and the raven, its principal aim is to introduce new or past authors—who have until now been marginalized—to an English-speaking readership. This series also highlights contemporary transnational authors, as well as writers who have never been translated or who are in need of a fresh/contemporary translation. The series further aims to increase the appreciation of translation as an art form that enhances the importance of cultural diversity.

This novel is the autobiographical story of the time a young boy spent in various orphanages in his native Russia, before being brought to Sicily, at the end of the novel, by his adoptive parents. Kola's/Nikolai's first-person narrative teems with cultural details of abuse, neglect, and destitution. In a world haunted by hardships and the absence of his parents, the presence of his older sister—housed in the same institution—and the infrequent visits of his aunt Babushka, are only a temporary salve. The compelling testimony that emerges from negotiating these situations and the transformations they require offers a harrowing yet tender glimpse of what it means to say farewell to a family, in all its fraught details, and a culture, even as a new one is formed.

For a complete list of titles in the **Other Voices of Italy** series, please see the last page in the book.

Farewell to Russia

Memories of When I Was Kola

Nikolai Prestia

Translated by Teresa Fiore
and Daniela Chaudhary Fiore

Foreword by Loredana Polezzi

RUTGERS UNIVERSITY PRESS
NEW BRUNSWICK, CAMDEN, AND NEWARK, NEW JERSEY
LONDON

Rutgers University Press is a department of Rutgers, The State University of New Jersey, one of the leading public research universities in the nation. By publishing worldwide, it furthers the University's mission of dedication to excellence in teaching, scholarship, research, and clinical care.

978-1-9788-4090-4 (cloth)
978-1-9788-4089-8 (paper)
978-1-9788-4091-1 (epub)

Cataloging-in-publication data is available from the Library of Congress.
LCCN 2025024462

British Cataloging-in-Publication record for this book is available from the British Library.

♾ The paper used in this publication meets the requirements of the American National Standard for Information Sciences—Permanence of Paper for Printed Library Materials, ANSI Z39.48-1992.

rutgersuniversitypress.org

You'll rediscover words
beyond the brief
nocturnal life of games,
beyond the glow of childhood.
It will be sweet to grow quiet.

—*Cesare Pavese, "You Are Also Hill,"*
October 30–31, 1945

Contents

Foreword

Why do we choose to read a book? To share it? Maybe to translate it? When we love a tale, we often recognize something in it, at times things we had not even been aware of before we started reading. *Farewell to Russia*, Nikolai Prestia's autobiographical novel first published as *Dasvidania* in Italy in 2021, pulls at deep-seated emotions. It asks us to recognize familiar feelings even as it takes us to unfamiliar places. It points to our sense of a common humanity just as it immerses us in the unique detail of a singular life story.

What you are about to read is a book about remembering. Memory opens like a window on the past, offering limited perspectives, partially obscured views, or, sometimes, suddenly clear, unrestricted vistas. Windows, real or imaginary, play an important part in the narrative. We repeatedly see the adult Nikolai sitting at his desk, writing, remembering, as the trees outside his room sway in the wind and shadows alternate with rays of light. He was always fascinated by windows, he tells us: by their sense of distance, of separation, mixed with the promise of privileged, first-row access to the world. We also see the young Kola sitting by a window in his shared orphanage bedroom, in the Russian city of Nizhny Novgorod. He is observing the world outside, trying to imagine an unimaginable future, but also to make sense of his present and not to forget his past, with the help of a solitary green apple that is itself the memory of a gift and a ghostlike memento of his mother.

Farewell to Russia is a book about childhood, or rather about memories of childhood. The writing is linear, deceptively transparent, as suits a narrative told through the eyes of a young boy. Yet this is a child who always was good at the (very serious) game of imagination. And, as the adult narrator tells us, children do understand what is going on in the world around them; they just do not have the words to explain it. Kola's early years were spent in the Russia of the 1990s, in the period following Chernobyl, the fall of the Berlin Wall, the collapse of the Soviet Union. There are signs, in these childhood memories, that Russia is opening up to the rest of the world: *Tom & Jerry* on the TV; the black Walkman proudly owned by an older boy. Yet Kola's landscapes are those of a decaying postindustrial world and a dissolving social structure. His neighborhood is ravaged by poverty, unemployment, alcohol, drugs, prostitution. Family ties are crumbling under the pressure of a generalized sense of loss, a vicious circle between the lack of escape routes into the future and an oppressive absence of any sense of aspiration. Those who resist (and there are some) offer a positive model made of simple gestures, dignified routines, deferred hopes. They are the adults Kola and his sister Alyona come to rely on, at least for short moments or brief spells of time: Babushka Faya, with her stout figure and the deep lines on her face; a great-grandmother who once baked a cake, turning Kola's birthday, for the first time, into a day of celebrations; a hospital nurse daring him to imagine a different, happier future; and a fatherly orphanage director who has Kola's same name, Nikolai Nikolajevich, and provides an alternative connection with a patronymic otherwise impossible to love or even to accept.

This is also a novel about solitude: the deep solitude of a child who never knew his father, lost his mother, is terrified of being separated from his sister. The childhood reconstructed in Nikolai Prestia's narrative is made of long silences, with the gaps between sections of the narrative serving as frequent reminders of that emptiness, the sense of void in the protagonist's life, as well as the untold and perhaps unremembered or unrememberable parts of the story. Then there are bursts of action, thrilling adventures, unexpected announcements, unforgettable admonishments, and gifts of wisdom. Nothing happens for what seems like forever, then suddenly one moment changes Kola's and Alyona's world, their entire life. Even when things do happen though, the ability to choose, to be in charge of one's own destiny, is still lacking. Irina, the children's mother, was from the beginning condemned never to have a choice, and so was her brother, the drug-addicted uncle who turns, for young Kola, into a real ogre.

Yet this is also a book about the good that comes from having a family, or from finding, inventing, recognizing multiple families. Brother and sister are family, of course, as are good aunts and great-grandmothers. But friends become family too, as they share the intimate details of their individual losses, the gaps left by the absence of love that need to be filled, every day, by a mix of proximity, trust, and respect for the defensiveness that hides in silence, for the need to be left alone at certain moments, in certain places. There is recognition toward the end in the encounter with those who will become Kola's new family, and that recognition is partly physical: one set of blue eyes lighting up a room as another used to. But for the most part, family is in gestures, in smiles, in kept promises, in the courage to make difficult choices, and in the ultimate generosity that allows an adult to acknowledge a child as their own even when they are not "blood of their blood." We see this first in Babushka Faya and then, especially, in the figure of the orphanage director, who calls the young boys and girls placed in his charge "figli della sua anima" (children of his soul). I don't know what the words for that expression would have been in Russian, as the director pronounced them, or what echoes they might carry in Russian culture. But reading them in Italian, today, it is almost impossible not to hear the voice of a much missed contemporary writer and public intellectual, Michela Murgia, with her defiant assertion that families are not only given but also found, searched for, invented, affirmed, through links that are not only, always, inevitably made of blood, but also of recognition, shared purpose, commitment, and trust.

Ultimately, *Farewell to Russia* is a book about loss, yes, but also and just as much a book about gain. We recognize the sadness and the silence of the orphan, afraid to lose even more than what he has already lost by making himself visible, by exposing himself to the world. We see the courage it takes to step out of an enclosed world made only of a shared bedroom, a familiar building, a snow-covered yard, a small hut from whose roof one can see an apple garden. It takes a lot of guts to keep nightmares at bay, or to dance for the first time with a girl. It takes even more guts to trust the words of adults, look them in the eye, rebel against their injustices, then eventually follow two of them all the way to a new home.

This, then, is a book about what's lost and found—which is also an excellent image of translation. The original version of the novel is written in Italian, with just a few transliterated Russian words emerging here and there in the text: the ambiguous title, *Dasvidania*, which is at once goodbye and so long; the name of a favorite childhood sweet, *sgushchjonnoe molokò*; not much else. But we know the story is told from memories first formed in Russian, shaped by Russian words (even though the author may no longer remember them). The first time we are meant to hear Italian—the first time Kola and Alyona hear that language—there is an interpreter, Alexsej, ready to mediate, to translate meanings and feelings across a linguistic divide that is not visible on the page, yet is still audible, palpable in the room where future parents and future children meet. He is another of the benign presences in the book, someone the children even dream of bringing with them as they leave Nizhny Novgorod and its snow for the South and the light of the Mediterranean. Like all other main and supporting actors in this story of childhood, Alexsej will be left behind—but not entirely erased or forgotten. And the same, it is tempting to think, may be true of Russia, its language, its culture.

Finally, what you are reading is not only a book built on translation but also a translated book. Each translation starts with a choice: an act of will through which we recognize a text as at least partly ours, then bring it into existence in another language, for another audience, in another place and, possibly, another time. The relationship between translator and text is close, intense, prolonged. It is intimate before it becomes public—but it is not necessarily lonely. In spite of a whole tradition that represents translators as hermits exclusively devoted to their task (just like their protector, Saint Jerome), more often than not translation is in fact collaborative: it involves editors, publishers, reviewers, . . . and frequently also cotranslators. This translation, the one you are going to read, was not a solitary effort, from the very beginning. It was produced *a quattro mani*, by a team made of mother and daughter, who each recognized something in Nikolai Prestia's book, felt it pull at their own emotions. As a result, this translation too is now part of the intricate geography of family ties that the novel both explores and constructs in front of our eyes. One gesture of hospitality inviting another. One leap of trust leading to the next. And one language layering its meanings, interweaving its traces with all the others.

Whether we spot them or not, in this translation there are (there must be: it cannot be otherwise) the traces of multiple languages and cultures. And they are even more numerous than those that already inhabit the original text. Besides the dialogue between Italian and English (the source and target languages), there is the lingering presence of Russian, hidden in plain sight in Kola/Nikolai's memories. Then there are other layers, more or less (in)audible, perhaps even unintentional: the Sicilian of the author and that of one of the translators; the Spanish(es) that are among the quotidian shared languages in the two translators' family. . . . And this is exactly how it should be, because families, languages, stories, and translations are made by and for those who care for them, live through them, and share them.

Loredana Polezzi, Stony Brook University (SUNY)

Translators' Note

In 2021 a friend aware of my story as an adoptive mother of a Colombian eight-year-old girl, Daniela, mentioned a book that had recently been published, *Dasvidania*, and whose author, Nikolai Prestia, was interviewed on a well-known radio program in Italy called *Fahrenheit*. The thematic focus of the book and the gentle but firm opinions expressed by Nikolai over the course of the interview convinced me that I needed to spend some time with *Dasvidania*. Often described as a book about adoption, *Dasvidania* is in reality the story of Kola journeying through a harrowing collection of early childhood experiences: a family life scarred by alcohol, heroin, violence, poverty, and prostitution in 1990s Russia eventually results in him and his sister navigating several orphanages. The adoption itself, when he is at the age of eight, only occurs toward the end of the book when an Italian couple takes the two siblings to Sicily to form a new family. The book—born as a diary and then turned into a hybrid mix of first-person memoir and autobiographical novel—is written in a simple language favoring parataxis, as is the general style of much Italian literature these days. Yet, the straightforward quality of the language is at odds with the profoundly complicated experience of Nikolai narrated in the book: neglect, abuse, destitution, anxiety, and depression, but also lyrical imagination, the ability to sublimate tragedy into poetic images, a willingness to denounce as much as to forgive, and certainly a determination to never forget, the reason why we have the book *Dasvidania*, now *Farewell to Russia: Memories of When I Was Kola*. With its positive outlook despite the dramatic quality of the childhood it narrates, the book is a testament to believing in new chapters of life. But perhaps even more strongly, it is a testament to believing in the power of writing as an act of translation of lived experience and of the self into words.

I eventually reached out to Nikolai and commenced a conversation with him that gradually moved beyond the content of the book or his path as a politically engaged emerging writer in Italy, and perhaps inevitably transformed into an exchange about adoption and the experience of being adopted with the baggage of a heavy childhood. He was in tune with the story of my daughter, as well as mine and that of my husband, even without knowing the details, which he learned about as part of a delicate dance of asking and intuiting. According to Nikolai, who in the meantime had become Niko since we grew closer, my daughter Daniela *had to* read his book in order to get a perspective on older adoptees' stories—a topic that is vastly underrepresented even in the literature of adoption—and mostly not to feel that her experience is/was so singular. The challenge, then, was to have her read the book . . .

In 2022 I invited Nikolai to present his book as part of the series of events that I organize on campus at Montclair State University in New Jersey, except that we were on Zoom, as was *de rigueur* in those days still affected by COVID-19. In preparation for the presentation, I thought about asking Daniela to translate some parts of the book for the event's webpage. Daniela is trilingual: Spanish is her first language, English is her main one after nine years of life in the United States, and Italian is her "mother tongue" in the literal sense of being the language she learned from me as her adoptive mother. Conversely, I became a mother in Spanish when my husband and I met her in Colombia; our family has been from the start a work of translation.

Daniela was into translating the book from the very start and over time met Niko on Zoom, curious as she was to speak to somebody who could put their childhood story of abandonment into words. When the Other Voices of Italy (OVOI) series came to life, and I had the honor of being invited to join the board, I enthusiastically suggested *Dasvidania* as a new title for the catalog along with more hesitantly proposing cotranslating it with Daniela. Alessandro Vettori championed this unorthodox partnership with a then fifteen-year-old from the beginning, and actually identified the multilingual and collaborative nature of the project as an enrichment of the series. His gesture of trust, further supported by the rest of the team at OVOI—Sandra Waters and Eilis Kierans—and eventually Rutgers University Press at large, has produced a sense of gratitude in me and Daniela that I can hardly translate (pun intended) into words.

This translated book has a unique aspect to it being both written and cotranslated by language migrants who have either moved to a new language, leaving one behind, or retained the languages of their transnational journeys. In particular, Nikolai and Daniela alike have embraced the language of their writing and translating, respectively, as part of the adoption process. They are in this book adoptees in their families as well as adopters of the language/s of their new families and countries. Nikolai's path into Italian has been paved by formal education but at the cost of the abrupt loss of his language, Russian, or rather a local dialect from the area of Nizhny Novgorod, which he identified as the language of trauma and, as such, something that was better forgotten. As a result, a childhood experience that took place in Russian was expressed for the first time in Italian in *Dasvidania*, in what is a form of unconscious translation for an exophonic writer. For Niko, who has read the Russian classics in Italian, this transition of his book into English is nothing short of a marvel. Daniela's acquisition of English as the language of adoption through schooling and socialization has also coincided with the acquisition of Italian in an osmotic way at home, through myself and my world, and has strongly leveraged her first language, Spanish. This is why she was able to translate the omnipresent "passato remoto" (simple past) in literature, one of the most difficult tenses for Italian-language learners, since she was seeing the Spanish "pretérito" in it, without even realizing it. For Daniela, this translation is a normal part of her plurilingual world, and yet a unique experience thanks to its ability to narrate what for her remains the unspeakable. And, she has grasped its core—as she simply but accurately put it—"You really do have a different connection with a book when you translate it. Because you do have to go in depth and really think about how it would be best translated: the more you get into the story, the better the translation will come out." I am trilingual myself as part of different forms of training and relocation across borders over the years, and I have translated essays in the past, but this is my first book. For me, as the cotranslator, editor, and project's weaver, this translation has been about the composition of a family, so to speak, sustained by words lost and found in translation. Echoing Salman Rushdie, I hope that Daniela and Niko will continue to gain much more than they have lost and that they will recognize their lives as a permanent act of translation: "We are translated [people]. It is normally supposed that something always gets lost in translation; I cling, obstinately, to the notion that something can also be gained" (17).

The translation process has worked at two levels, then, one synchronic in terms of overlapping languages and one diachronic in terms of phases involving different actors, including Nikolai himself through numerous WhatsApp messages. Daniela's pace followed the flow of the life of a teenager: at times the book received uninterrupted attention, at others it came to a halt due to unexpected turns of life, and at yet others it had to be squeezed in between simultaneous commitments. On average, it essentially followed a routine of one page a day for two years. The translation became another family member; it grew with us. Daniela dove into the project, handwriting the translation on paper sheets, which I have scanned as a memento, to then move to the computer and, to a degree, the translation technology it affords. Yet her excitement about it soon gave way to a new awareness. She discovered how limiting these artificial tools can be since they cannot tell "she" from "he" in a sentence with no explicit subject in Italian. Further confusion ensued when Kola was identified as a woman due to the final "a." In this sense, Daniela came to the same conclusion as the writer Liz McSkeane: "Literal translation, perhaps supported by technology . . . might help with this . . . process of recasting an entire work of literature in another language; . . . but it cannot do the work that needs to be done." Daniela learned to do the work, to reread and adapt, and was particularly keen on becoming attuned to the soundscape of the novel by way of memory. "I often translated by re-imagining scenes from the orphanage in my head," she explained one day. Mostly, she opted for slangish solutions in the conversations among the children: "This is how abandoned kids talk, Mom: they are not afraid of offending each other. Life has offended them."

The vocabulary of the book seldom posed challenges, and even proverbs and expressions we were able to render fairly easily. Some terms were translated in more than one form. In the original text, the word "istituto" refers to the orphanage, and the author privileged it over the more literal "orfanotrofio" since, as he explained to us, in an orphanage abandoned children with living (single) parents often outnumber actual orphans. To respect his choice but also in the interest of more realistically rendering the experience of the children in this socially connoted place, we translated it alternatively as "institute" (building) and "orphanage" (lived space). We switched between "children" and "kids" to refer to "bambini" depending on the in/formality of the context. We used both "gypsy" and "Roma" to refer to a nickname and the ethnic origin of a character, respectively. And we retained "faggot" for "finocchio" rather than use the more politically correct "gay," given the offensive attitude of the speaker in a couple of instances. Overall, the text adopts a more formal tone in descriptions and when educated adults are talking, and a more colloquial one for children. A truly challenging aspect of the text is its interwoven double register. While told from the point of view of a child—Kola in the book—the story is conveyed by a thirty-plus-year-old exophonic writer—Nikolai—who has a law degree and allows himself, perhaps inadvertently, to include more sophisticated turns of phrases that a child would not use. This is another characteristic that we tried to preserve ("imprimatur" for "benestare" is an instance of this loftier vocabulary).

Ultimately, it was the punctuation that required the most decision-making. With its asyndetic style, *Farewell to Russia: Memories of When I Was Kola* is a text replete with commas, as if the events, places, and people narrated were a chain of connections rather than self-standing entities marked by endings. Nikolai's perspective: "The final period is a forceful intervention, while the comma reflects a mental rhythm that extends the emotion in what is effectively a flow of consciousness." Daniela and I opted for including a certain number of final periods, colons, and semicolons, trying to find a balance between the author's original intention and the necessary readability of the text for Anglophone readers. Daniela's reaction: "Why do I have to use 'proper' punctuation in my homework if a prize-winning author can ignore it?"

As for the method, Daniela made the choice of translating the book as she read it, perhaps a typical attitude of adolescents who live in the moment, I thought initially, only to be pleasantly surprised by discovering that Julio Cortázar's translator, Gregory Rabassa, used the same approach, as Andrew Bast recounts: "Without having read [*Rayuela* (*Hopscotch*)] . . . [he] sat down and typed a draft in English, word by word," and followed this practice with Gabriel García Márquez's *One Hundred Years of Solitude* as well. Rabassa himself recalls: "I knew it was a damn good book, but it wasn't as much fun knowing all about it"; so he typed it as he read it, page by page.[1] Almost every night, Daniela sent me a page of translation with words and expressions she was unfamiliar with highlighted in yellow, and my task as partial cotranslator was to compare the original, entertain an exchange with her about the alternatives, and then wait for the next installment, like Shahryar for Scheherazade. Once the entire book was completed, I embarked on in-depth editing with the precious assistance of Stephanie Jed, my former Ph.D. mentor, and eventually on the official editing process with the OVOI team.

Over the months and ultimately years, Daniela has remained aware of the unique nature of the opportunity she was given, even as her attachment to the project waxed and waned due to the nature of adolescence and the arduous journey of identification and distancing that translating this book required: "It's a really tragic story with many hard things to process but in the end something good did come out of it. I connected a lot to this story and many sections were very painful to read because I would think back to memories that I don't want to think about. The book really hit me hard in several passages to the point that I had to stop and reread . . . which doesn't happen often to me." If Niko's book suggests the cathartic function of writing through the unearthing of trauma, its translation makes us wonder about the further amplification of this function, without necessarily reducing it to a therapeutic cliché. True, only 3 percent of the book market in the United States is made up of translated books, and inside it the presence of adoption stories from abroad, and even more so of older adoptees' stories, is extremely limited.[2] Yet, the publication of *Dasvidania* in English with the potential of reaching numerous Anglophone countries around the globe in the future can hopefully represent an important step in building the circuit for this amplifier.

Ultimately, Niko and Daniela have "written" *Dasvidania* in English together, indirectly sharing wounds and experiences that aged them prematurely. As the weaver of their exchange and editor of their words, I feel like a boatwoman who has carried them from one side of the river to the other, as they traveled together without being physically on the same river. Yet, come to think of it, a more suitable metaphor surfaces. Years ago, during a trip to Colombia, we stopped in Montería, a town known for its rafts taking people from one side of the Sinú River to the other through the simple force of currents and some ropes. These rafts—called *planchones*—are fundamental to the life of the city; yet they are not part of the public transportation system. They are privately owned, and thus decorated according to the style of those who have built them and drive them, as if they were their little houses. In a sense, I have acted as a *planchón* in this project, a little house built by Niko first and Daniela later that has traveled between (two) languages.

Teresa Fiore with contributions
from Daniela Chaudhary Fiore

NOTES

1. I am grateful to Peter Constantine for pointing this source out to me at the American Association of Teachers of Italian conference in Catania, Sicily, in 2023 at a roundtable devoted to OVOI / Rutgers University Press.

2. See Three Percent: A Resource for International Literature at the University of Rochester, "About," accessed July 20, 2025, https://www.rochester.edu/College/translation/threepercent/about.

WORKS CITED

Bast, Andrew. "A Translator's Long Journey, Page by Page." *New York Times*, May 25, 2004. https://www.nytimes.com/2004/05/25/books/a-translator-s-long-journey-page-by-page.html.

McSkeane, Liz. "Gabriel Garcia Márquez and the Alchemy of Translation." Turaspress.ie, June 28, 2022.

Rushdie, Salman. "Imaginary Homelands." In *Imaginary Homelands: Essays and Criticism 1981–1991*, 9–21. New York: Penguin, 1991.

Farewell to Russia

~

Quiet, with the face of an angel and always downcast. Golden hair that looked like stalks of wheat, but soft to the touch like wool in winter. Kola was his name.

Word was that he couldn't speak. Asocial, he couldn't stand the other kids in the orphanage. It felt like he wasn't even there. Only during meals would you be able to see the lifeblood flowing through his body: he chewed quickly and with a slight breathlessness. You could recognize, but not always, his tone of voice when he asked: "Another slice of bread, sir, please." It was so rare to hear him speak that his voice came across as a gift: it was very sweet, like that of all children his age.

———

The orphanage is a pale gray ugly building, so pale that it disappears into the snow during winter. More tall than wide, it accommodates about eighty young orphans in twenty rooms, each of the same size. Each room is furnished with four beds and two closets. There is also a carpet, one of those colorful carpets donated by foundations. Winter in Russia is harsh: one cold draft of air and ice begins to form, even on heating units working full blast, and the carpets become necessary allies. The building is an old barracks adapted to provide a home for street children. On the ground floor, in the workshops, from six in the evening until before dinner, the children participate in recreational activities: there is a darkroom, an art studio, and a woodshop, Kola's favorite. On the ground floor there is also a welcoming cafeteria, with twenty-two tables, two of which are reserved for the staff. Then there is the office of the director, a calm fatherly man. His name is Nikolai Nikolajevich: prematurely a widower, he spends a lot of time with "the children of his soul," as he calls them.

The furniture on the first floor is reduced to the bone: large green doors leading to the rooms open out on a corridor that looks like a river. At each end of the corridor, there is a plant that grows only in winter and appears to die in summer, when the institute empties out with the children leaving for summer camp.

The institute is located at the center of a large square. A huge garden grows in front of the building, with trees and berry plants. To the right of the garden there is a small soccer field. And swings and slides that in winter are swallowed up by snow and frost.

The back of the building looks out on the old town. If you breathe toward the sky, in the distance you can see the smoke of the factories, where some of the children dream of working one day, to create the family they didn't have, or that they had for a short and hard time.

Facing the institute is a school that takes kids through high school graduation. Education is a serious thing, as the director always reminds them. Their future rests on education: what is lost can be made up and, even if you don't make it up, a new opportunity, a new life is always possible. School is the place Kola hates the most, even though he's good at math.

And this is how I imagine myself being described in the third person, while I light up a cigarette and observe the pencil drawing of a horse hanging on my bedroom wall. This is how I remember that place. Kola was me. Kola *is* me.

I was born in Nizhny Novgorod, an important city in Russia, bordered by the Volga River. I remember the sky: ocean blue in the nearby countryside and dark gray on the streets, a blend of snow, smog, and melancholy. I always used to stare at the sky. As I grew up, I got out of the habit, but I still stare sometimes.

And I wonder, now as then: What does that sky do with the stars? Make a wish? Is it the sky that makes them fall? I would like to have some happy memories, but now, as I write and smoke the last cigarette of the pack, I'm unable to bring any into focus.

Irina and Alyona, two very common names in Russia. Alyona is my sister. Irina is the woman who brought us into this world. She became a mother without much awareness: she was nineteen when she gave birth to my sister, and twenty when I was born. I have just a few memories of her but one thing I can say with absolute certainty is that she was gorgeous. Blue eyes like the sky when the sun is happy; wavy and straw-colored hair just like mine when I was a child. She was wrapped in sorrow, perpetually unable to choose. The men around her understood this. My mother supported herself through prostitution. It was a difficult life: drugs and alcohol, beatings and strong smells, men. Many men, and all the abuse that followed for both her and us.

Now that I'm taking the last hit of my cigarette, a sweet memory comes to mind. One Sunday morning it seemed like Irina wanted to change her life. She arranged the furniture in a new way; she seemed happy. Or at least I thought so. She was even more beautiful than usual. She managed to fix the old TV and we watched *Tom & Jerry* together. She was sitting on the bed and I was on her lap. She would push me away, leaving me to shiver in the void, and then pull me in again making me feel safe in her grasp. We softly kissed each other on the lips and she repeated to me, "Ya tebya lyublyu," which means "I love you." She was wearing an elegant dress, dark blue with a large checkerboard of red and light blue shades. It felt like the fabric kissed her face, ready to take her—the most beautiful woman in town—to a dance. When I look at the sky, I always think of her. And when that happens, I imagine I am reliving that moment. Sometimes I feel like saying to her: run away, leave me and Alyona behind, we will be fine. Run away: you don't have a chance there. But it is a moment that I can't make real, life has gone its way, I have gone my way, and Irina—briefly and with no alternative route—her way.

This memory is also precious to me because it was the last day Irina and I were happy together.

The next morning—at least I think it was the next morning—Faya, the aunt that my sister and I always called Babushka, took us to an orphanage. I remember crying and hating her. I was tearing out my hair, every gesture and intense cry filled with despair.

It's like planting a seed: you sink it there, in the dark underground, and you pour water on it, and you seem to forget about it. The seed, if it had a soul, would hate you. Because it doesn't understand. The seed has never seen a tree, a flower, or a small plant sprout from the ground. If we were all born with a healthy dose of experience, we would hate less and understand more.

"Babushka, why are you leaving us here? Take us with you," we repeated, as the awareness of our abandonment started to sink in. With experience, over the years, we would understand that her action caused her much pain, but was also the seed of our new life.

During my childhood I lived in three orphanages. In the first one, there were only twenty kids, with different stories and the same destiny: that heavy feeling that we didn't have a place in this world. As kids, we understand things, it's only that we aren't able to give shape and order to our thoughts. Fear and anguish dig inside of us forever. In this very small building, we could play and have a warm meal, but Mom wasn't there.

The walls of orphanages all have the same dull shade. Even when there is a rainbow painted on the walls, the colors don't sparkle, the fog of abandonment turns off the light in the kids' eyes. It turned mine off too. When everything looked dark, Alyona brought back the light. My sister is a year older than I am, though you couldn't tell just by looking at us. She has always been a little shorter than me. Back then, she had short hair, with a bob haircut that made her look carefree. Big eyes the color of dark hazelnuts, able to absorb the premature blows of life. A serious look, a little like mine. But her sparkling smile could light up a dark, windowless room. Those standing beside her in those happy moments were certain to feel a primordial warmth bathing their chests. Of course, we fought as kids. And she often stripped off my flesh with those nails that she let grow in her rush to become a young woman. Our fights were like the beginning of an eternal feud, an uncontained explosion of layered anger. Usually, she would win because she didn't care about the damage she inflicted. She had small ears and a slightly protruding nose that gave her a comical appearance. I often wondered, without daring to ask her, if she would ever be able to think about her future with serenity. Who knows if we had the same dreams—mostly nightmares. We didn't have an actual dialogue: we were still too young to truly understand the meaning of being siblings related by blood. When one of us perceived a change in the air, or even when a bedroom door slammed in a particularly violent way, our eyes would meet: maybe this is what it means to be siblings, to ignore each other when things are normal and to look for and know each other in moments of uncertainty, when fear makes you vulnerable. Seeing her next to me in that place forsaken by a good God gave me strength. I promised myself that they would never separate us.

I never socialized with the kids in this place. Inside those walls something happened that really shook me. There was this Roma kid, very lively and, I must admit, adorable. He was able to connect with one of the three teachers, the most beautiful one. She always wore colorful clothes to cheer us up, to conceal the city's gray sky from us. One day everyone—kids and teachers alike—shared the dreams they had the night before. I had dreamed of a toy car that said, "I am yours." To this day I still remember the excitement and fear that I felt in hearing the dream of the Roma kid and the weird coincidence that followed. He was on a street, a very dark street, he couldn't hear anything and he felt his world begin to spin. His mom appeared to him and, all of a sudden, he found himself in a hospital room. All by himself, abandoned even by the staff. The building was completely empty and there was a strange, frightening echo in the corridors. The echo made its way into his mouth, and suddenly everything went quiet; the Roma kid was screaming but not a sound could be heard. All of a sudden, he woke up. The dream itself was very strange, even macabre, considering that the dreamer was a seven-year-old. But what really disturbed me was the teacher's reaction: on hearing the story, she became pale. She seemed frightened; I couldn't understand why. At that time, I was convinced that adults were never afraid. Everything became clear when it was the teachers' turn to speak. The first two told made-up dreams that sounded like fairy tales by improbable writers with unlikely circumstances and a moral tacked on at the end. When it was the beautiful teacher's turn, we sensed something strange in the air. My sister and I huddled closer. "I was walking down the street, a very dark street. I couldn't hear anything but I felt the world spinning. All of a sudden, I found myself in the hallway of a hospital; I could hear a noise that wanted to explode but was suppressed. I started running and found the little Roma kid and hugged him. He called me 'Mom.' And I woke up." When she stopped talking, the Roma kid was scared, and one after the other, so were we all. How was it possible that they were in the same dream? For me it was absurd: the life I was living was not real, there was no way one could look for foundations and certainties in dreams. The teacher explained to us that sometimes we can find ourselves in a dream with someone we desire strongly. I was shocked and asked myself if one of them was in love with the other.

I don't have many memories of this first orphanage, it was calm, small, and cozy in the cold winter time.

After a few months, my sister and I were transferred to another orphanage. I don't have many recollections of that place either. We were there for a few weeks. But in that short time, it felt as if life had slapped me, my uncertain certainty collapsed, and pain, starting from the tip of my toes, traversed my entire body and settled in my chest, leaving me forever melancholy.

In that period, Babushka came to see us. Alyona and I were really happy to be able to spend a little time with her. Her presence meant that she had not abandoned us. Hearing the teachers say "Kola and Alyona, come. There is a visitor for you" was like receiving a piece of candy. Irina, our mother, also came for a visit. I was so happy to see her again, I couldn't imagine that it would be the last time. We went to the visiting room and found her there with a black eye, tears, and a little bag of green apples. One of those apples was rotten. I remember this scene with pain, while I look for something in the sky through my bedroom window, hidden behind a cypress blowing in the wind. I couldn't understand why Irina was crying, I tried to hug her, and her tears turned into explosive sobs. I backed away quickly, convinced I had made things worse. I could smell the stench of that rotten apple filling the entire room, my right leg was shaking, I was frightened. Alyona kept quiet. What I told myself in the years afterward was that Irina needed a longer hug. Or, perhaps blaming myself makes me feel better, so that every time I think of that day, I give Irina a chance to escape, to relieve her of her bad choices, her lack of courage. But as much as I try to relive that moment again, to attempt to radically change every tiny detail to the point of confusing the past with the present and thought with reality, the truth is that I can't change anything. I can only accept that the day went the way it did. It is a tremendous strain, like wearing, in the summer, ten heavy jackets made out of "if's," "maybe's," and "but's" that keep me from breathing until I stop thinking about Irina. Every time it's a struggle: my childhood is enclosed in an eternal "I should have." Irina was quiet, didn't say a thing, she was sitting there with her little bag of apples. An hour passed before she left. She told us she loved us a lot. She burst into tears again and walked away leaving the little bag on the chair. The last memory I have of her smell is of the smoke on her clothes, along with that of alcohol that spread through the room and covered the stench of the rotten apple.

Two weeks later, on a cold morning, while I was playing with toy cars, Alyona approached me. She had a melancholy air about her and teary eyes. She told me that she had dreamed about our mother's death. I replied saying that it was just a dream and that bad dreams never come true. Only the good ones, what you really wish for, come true. I reminded her about the dream of the teacher and the Roma kid, telling her that dreams are unreal and reflect our desires, and that desires are only beautiful things. Alyona contradicted me, but I continued to insist: desires are beautiful things, hard to reach and this is why we dream about them. And when the desire is so strong, a star falls from the sky, and right then everything comes true. We don't desire bad things, we fear them. And this is why bad dreams don't come true: we don't desire them.

She smiled faintly and went back to playing with the other girls.

It took just a few words, as if it were an ordinary matter. My sister and I were taken to an empty room and in the starkest silence they informed us of the death of our mother. The silence in the room turned to noise. My screams and sobs filled every wall, every corner. It couldn't be true. I had never experienced the death of anyone I knew, death for me was something ugly but unreal. I couldn't imagine a body existing without life. But I was discovering death through my mother, the same woman through whom I discovered life. My scream was the same as back then, when I looked out at this world for the first time. After those words were uttered, I was no longer myself. I stopped smiling. I started to fear everything: people, dogs, shadows, songs, contact.

I had barely anything, just a mother with problems, and life took even that away. Who would protect me now? Who would console me after a nightmare? Obviously, Irina wasn't an attentive person, but deep down I hoped that one day she could change and notice Alyona and me. When Irina died, the hope of something beautiful died with her. The next few days I was constantly at the window, where I observed people walking on the other side of the street; or, when it wasn't cold and you could open the windows for a few minutes, I entertained myself by guessing, from the sound that they made, the models of the cars that passed. I was always wrong. But it didn't matter. I had lost everything and not even my sister was able to change my mood. Now that our mother had passed away, who would take care of my sister? And if I weren't around, where would she go? And there were also tears of hate. Yes, hate. I hated Alyona because she was my sister, because she had been my first experience of love, that sibling love that lasts for a lifetime, and she was *my* sister. The sister of a coward prone to tears. And we were the children of a distracted woman with an unhappy life. Wouldn't it be better if she had been the sister of someone else, with a respectable family? I detested my mother as well. Why didn't she tell me that we were hugging each other for the last time? Adults know everything. At least that's what I believed at the time.

Time passed slowly, listlessly. Maybe time was tired of never being enough for anybody: everybody was always asking for "a little more, a little bit more," even if it was already too late. When things don't go the way they should and we don't want to feel this burden, we look for someone to blame. That's it, the function of time for me was to swallow the worst in life, to endure insults and offense.

But all of a sudden, everything started to move, things began to unfold fast, perhaps a little too fast. We were informed that soon we would move to another institute and that it would be different. We would live with older children, and I was very happy; I thought it would be a way of getting to know the world through the eyes of those with just a little more experience.

That moment came on a sunny autumn day in which the rays of the sun revealed the cracks in buildings. At the time, the city was full of wide streets and large buildings. All of the buildings had the same shape with sad and dull-colored tiles tired of holding themselves together. The wood of the entrance doors was rotten, eaten away by the dreams of beggars sheltering there during the coldest nights. The trees were beautiful, tall, very tall, with wide leaves. To me the streets were all alike and useless: in any case, even if I wanted to go somewhere, I couldn't. On sunny days, you could find ice cream vendors on the streets, and the ice cream was really tasty. The vendors went around with heavy, shiny iron carts. At least I thought they were heavy, because the vendors struggled to push them or, maybe, they were tired, sad, and disappointed, even though they always tasted the sweet side of life. When we left this second institute, the teachers offered each of us an ice cream. Mine was gone in the blink of an eye, while my sister savored the moments of sweetness, letting the ice cream melt on her clothes. The sun brightened up the city, the cars were speeding in all directions, and I stared at my own reflection in the window of the vehicle, headed toward the umpteenth new old destination. It was a loud bus filled with kids. Initially, we didn't understand, but at the first stop realized that we were being transferred to different institutes. That's when I started shaking. My worst nightmare was about to come true. What if I ended up alone? What if they were to separate Alyona and me? I couldn't breathe, I wanted to cry but I couldn't. Kids who cry in front of other kids are signing their own sentences: teasing and indifference are sure to follow. We had to be strong, or at least pretend to be strong. Everybody pretended, always: the adults with their kindnesses and the children who, in order to receive a little pity, expressed their fears without emotion. At every stop I held my breath, I stared at the social worker, and my heart stopped beating. Then, the doors closed again, the driver—vague and distracted—stepped on the gas and the bus started up again. My heart would also start again, as Alyona and I were fleeing from the risk of being separated. After three stops, I heard someone utter my sister's name. It was like dying in an instant. Silence came to visit me, the same silence as in the room where I found out about Irina's death. I understood nothing of what the social worker was mumbling until a little kid made me move with kicks and insults. I also got off in front of that institute: I was still with my sister. In that moment, her name seemed to contain all the happiness that fate can offer to human beings.

And here we are at the entrance to a new place. The door seemed to disappear into the grayish facade of this large building. I was scared. Alyona was there ready, as always, to accept the changes. The director came to welcome us, a man with broad shoulders, his face hidden by a thick black beard that was starting to turn gray. He had deep, light-colored eyes and a contagious smile, deliberately refined over time to be displayed when it was time to welcome the new arrivals. He looked at us, stroked our hair, and he explained, smiling: "This place won't be your home but your last orphanage. Here you will find older kids who will help you grow, and I am sure you will like it here. There will be three attendants at your disposal, one of whom is outstanding in math. Obviously now you two are old enough to go to school. The school is across the street, all you have to do is walk there to advance toward your future. I am the director, but don't let this word scare you: I am only a director for bureaucratic purposes; otherwise, I am your teacher, custodian, cook, and—why not—also your friend. Welcome." He concluded the conversation with another smile. He had a warm, deep, and welcoming voice. And I felt as if I had finally arrived at the right place.

We stood there for another minute or so. Looking around, Alyona and I were drawn toward the immense garden full of trees, while the director spoke with the social worker about matters related to our arrival. Before leaving, he smiled at us without saying anything. Shortly after, two of the attendants arrived. They were also smiling and young. One was blond with dark highlights and a very funny haircut. She looked like a poodle. The second one had really short dark hair. They told us something before showing us around, but I don't remember what.

Stepping inside, our eyes were immediately drawn to the large aquarium right in the middle of the long and narrow hallway on the ground floor. It was full of fish and it was really beautiful. I had never seen fish swim in an aquarium; they were all green with silvery fins that gleamed with radiance against the glass. One of the attendants started to explain the institute's layout. Right after the aquarium, continuing down the hallway, there was the door to a large room filled with showers. They told us that we should shower once a week. Further down, there were three blue doors. Those were the rooms for recreational workshops: one for art, one for photography, and the last one for carpentry. The workshops were a surprise to me; it really seemed like this new place would be able to distract me from all those dark thoughts that are unfit for children. We reached the end of the corridor and turned right, going down three stairs and stepping into the cafeteria. It was huge with a light brown color enveloping the walls and tables. On one side there was a window that connected the kitchen and the dining room. The tables were already set. The attendants told us there were four meals a day. Breakfast was at eight, lunch at one, a snack at five, and dinner at eight. They advised us to always be punctual. I thought it was pointless advice. Kids like me and Alyona suffered from three things: loneliness, coldness, and hunger. We went up the stairs and found ourselves on the first floor, the one with the bedrooms. The hallway was completely empty, you could only hear the sound of our steps. The light that entered through the large windows at both ends wasn't strong. They showed us our rooms. Mine was really close to the attendants' room, while my sister's was at the other end. Boys and girls stayed in different areas separated by the bathrooms. It was the first time ever that my sister and I were apart from each other. It was a strange sensation, everything was strange. I have always been hostile to changes, to novelty. After smiling at my sister and agreeing on a time for lunch, I stepped into my new room. There were four fairly large wooden beds. On the floor there was the typical worn-out carpet to make the surroundings more welcoming and, next to the wall, a closet. On my bed, the second to the left close to the window, I found the school uniform. A green sweater with a geometric pattern, a white shirt, and a pair of brown flannel pants. I felt lonely and wondered where the others were. Who knows what Alyona was up to. I fell asleep and was awakened an hour later by the clamor of the kids returning from school. I started fretting: I was scared but also curious to meet my roommates. There they were: Ivan, Arthur, and Sasha. The first two were much older than me: they welcomed me without even asking what my name was. Sasha seemed more interested. He asked my name and age, and told me I could sit next to him at lunch. I smiled, happy. The presence of Arthur and Ivan made me nervous. Arthur was a dark-skinned boy with black, greasy hair. His nose was prominent and disjointed with a conspicuous bump. He had large eyes that made his gaze unsettling; his very presence caused tension. Ivan was tall and muscular with very short hair. He appeared to know everything, he treated everyone with arrogance, and he walked around as if he were God knows who. Sasha, on the other hand, was my same age with really fair skin, covered with beauty marks all over his arms and one on his face. He was also blond, like me, and smiled sweetly, conveying serenity. Around one in the afternoon the bell rang. We set off toward the stairs. The hallways

I had seen empty were now full of kids and colliding voices. It felt like a subway car. On the stairs, the kids promptly formed a line, everyone was staring at me: some were saying, "That's the new kid," and others were laughing at me. All of a sudden, I heard some people calling Sasha. They were two of his friends, who also introduced themselves right away: Mishka and Sergej. They were smiling, joking around, and tried to include me in their conversations. While we were going down the last set of stairs, a redheaded boy grabbed my arm and said to me while laughing aggressively: "You won't last here very long without crying." Sergej intervened right away, ordering him to let go of my arm and to never speak to me again with that tone of voice. He told him I was his friend. I felt so many conflicting emotions: fear as well as courage, shyness but at the same time a desire to get to know my three new friends. Before going into the cafeteria I saw my sister again: she looked calm, she was chatting with two girls, she didn't even notice me. I was happy with that; it meant she was feeling at ease. We all sat down at the table after walking past the kitchen window, where the cooks had filled our plates. Pasta with cabbage, this was today's lunch. Once we were all seated, the director came in. He had us pray and, before wishing us "bon appétit," introduced me and my sister to everyone else. He urged them to treat us well. When he was done talking, a welcoming applause from the group added color to my face. We started eating, I was happy. The meal was good and in front of me, two tables away, I caught a glimpse of my sister.

As I took my eyes off of her, I noticed Ivan's arrogant look and malicious smile. He said something to Arthur, who looked at me in the same way. I didn't understand the meaning of those looks until later when we finished eating and went back to our rooms. I felt anxious going up the stairs, every step was like a boulder. In previous institutes, there was often talk of hazing: older kids had to show the younger ones how things worked and to whom they were expected to show respect. At the top of the stairs, where the smell of cabbage soaked into the walls of the hallway, I heard someone call me: "Hey newbie, wait up!"

I didn't move, it felt like the whole world had also stopped moving. A tingling sensation ran down from my arms to the tips of my fingers. Although I had only heard that voice a few times, I could still sense its deceitful vibration. My feeling was confirmed, when I saw that Ivan and Arthur had just walked into my room. Only then did I notice that Sasha, Sergej, and Mishka weren't there, they had already abandoned me on the stairs. I started shaking, trying to hide my fear from the two of them. Arthur said: "Come on, what are you doing outside in the hall? Step in, we have to talk to get to know each other better." Ivan smiled viciously, guarding the door like a pole, a sentry. Arthur lit up a cigarette. He didn't quite know how to hold it, looked awkward, wanted to seem older than he was. He took a hit and choked on it; that made him nervous. He cursed and ordered me to sit on the bed in front of the chair he was comfortably sitting on. He started speaking to me.

"So, where are you from?" I replied, "I wouldn't know, I come from another orphanage, I have never had a real home and the neighborhood my mom lived in was full of gray and very tall buildings." I continued the conversation asking, "And you?" But he just looked at me, called Ivan over and started laughing. "How about this? Now he's the one asking the questions." I clenched my hands together, they felt frozen as if ice had gotten into my veins. Arthur changed his tone, sat more calmly, with his arms supporting a face that appeared heavy, full of anger. He looked at me: "Of course! I know where you come from. I have been in that neighborhood. I go every time I have permission to go out. I choose a woman, we do what we have to do and if she insists that I have to pay, all I have to do is take out this knife." Instantly, like magic, a red pocketknife with a button appeared in his hands. He pressed that little button and using the same sly tone, said to me: "You see this blade? It is the only certainty I have! It is thanks to this blade that I can sleep calmly at night. Words and good manners have no use. Maybe in America but not here. Here you always need to complement your words with a knife. And this blade is still a virgin, I have never needed to use it. It has the same function as words, only it is more sincere. It allows us to be clear with the world. Don't be scared, I see you peeing in your pants, and I bet you're thinking about that slutty mother of yours, but she isn't here! She is too busy fucking strangers to be able to cuddle you. All mothers are the same. They fuck, have kids, and instead of raising them, they send them to an orphanage. Only a strong man makes them feel good. Who wants a kid? A kid doesn't even amount to the leg of a man: a kid is only a waste of time and much effort. I was also a kid once and now that I am older, things haven't changed." Listening to these words, my heart became a frozen lake, I was the ugly-duckling outcast. I wanted to cry but I couldn't. I missed my mother, I wished she were here. Arthur's words weren't true. They couldn't be true. The more I thought about my mother the sadder I became. At that moment I realized that I would never see her again. It was like realizing she was dead through the bitter sound of Arthur's words.

Ivan intervened pointedly: "Where did you put my cologne?" I thought: Me, cologne? I rarely took a shower and didn't even know that soap was used for washing and now Ivan was asking me about cologne. My hesitation annoyed Arthur, who took me by the arm and asked me in a threatening voice: "Hey, why aren't you answering? There is no room here for thieves. We already have nothing and if we do get something, we have to thank heaven. So, find the cologne right away." I didn't understand that it was a trap. A pretext for giving me a welcome, which arrived immediately. Ivan punched me in the ribs, the kind of punch that hurts. The kind that life has to give you to prepare you for the wretchedness of the world, to convince you that there's no use hoping for things to get better. That punch hurt less for the impact than for its meaning. I was alone, incapable of either defending or absolving myself of something I didn't do. Arthur punched me in the face. I almost fainted. I remember this scene like it was yesterday. I was smelling Arthur's skin, it seemed like he hadn't bathed. It was the taste of reality that surrounded me. I started to cry, and when I shed the first tear, the final blow came: a punch to the chest. This time, I swear, the world really stopped. My lungs and heart stopped. I felt like how a fish probably feels right after being caught and hurled to the ground to stop its fins from moving. I wanted to take a breath but I couldn't; I had a bitter candy stuck in my throat or maybe it was a rock. It had a bad taste. I felt the pressure rising in my head, my eyes wanted to pop out, escaping from me and reality. Arthur and Ivan got scared, they made me lie down immediately all the while insulting each other. One said there was no need to go overboard and that, after all, I was so much younger. They started telling me: "Kola, Kola, breathe. If you don't breathe, we will kill you for real and you won't see your sister ever again." As soon as I heard these last words, I started breathing, with pain, but I was alive. Alive like I have always been, with a dull, melancholic ache that right now felt like a sharp pang in my chest. Arthur looked at me and said: "Did you learn your lesson? If the attendants find out about this, you'll get the rest of what's coming to you, but with a belt because you are not even worthy of a scratch from my knife. A scar would be like an adornment to your face." They spat on me and left. I remained there on the bed, who knows for how long. I felt the heat of the mattress and realized too late that I had wet myself and that the smell of my pee had filled the room.

And there I was, a seven-year-old with a bloody nose and pain in my chest staring into space. A perfect snapshot of me and my life. I was alone, as before, but this time I had the feeling that loneliness would be my life's companion. Now, remembering and reliving that day, I realize that the loneliness I felt back then was a wish: it would have been much better to be alone than with Ivan and Arthur in the orphanage.

Half an hour later, my three friends came to the room. They didn't look me in the eye, they just said sorry. I understood they had been told not to show up until after I had received my welcome. They wished they were a few years older so that they could have defended me, since they too had undergone that ritual. Mortified, Sasha came closer and gave me a chocolate bar. He told me his mom had brought it two days earlier. It was the kind gesture I was looking for, and I decided to share the bar with everybody. We started talking, I don't remember what was said. I was still dazed but we talked about everything except what had just happened. I wouldn't receive that treatment again unless I failed to respect the older kids. That afternoon flew by thanks to the company of my new friends.

I stayed in my room for dinner, I wasn't hungry and I wanted to be alone and get used to the idea that people born in neighborhoods like mine aren't allowed to dream of beauty. Now, even when I'm happy, if I think of that day again, I get goosebumps, and a sadness settles inside of me. Each time, it is hard to let go of that punch to the chest. It's as if it sentenced me to a lifetime of melancholy, to a pause of silent darkness, even in the midst of light and sound.

~

It was seven thirty. The attendants knocked and walked into our rooms to wake us up. I pretended not to understand what was happening. I didn't want to go to school, not after what had happened the day before. Sasha was already dressed and showed off his contagious smile. He prodded me to get dressed quickly and to brush my teeth. In the blink of an eye, I was ready . . . to have breakfast, not to go to school. At the bottom of the stairs, Mishka and Sergej were waiting for us. They greeted me and told me to hurry up. We had a large satisfying breakfast. In Russia, breakfast is an important meal. In our cafeteria, a milk soup with pasta was served during autumn and winter. Warm milk and pasta are necessary to combat the cold; without them it's impossible to walk out and endure the snow. They also served each of us an apple. A green apple, my favorite. I hid it in the backpack that one of the attendants had given me the night before. They also gave me two books, some pencils and pens. After breakfast, we got in line, two by two, with an attendant at the head. We walked through the garden along a path of trodden grass, trampled over for years until it no longer wanted to grow. It looked like a large dragon stretched out for sunbathing. Even from the windows of the institute you could see this little trail with its faded color. It was barely visible in spring and early autumn but disappeared altogether in winter. The dragon went into hibernation.

At the far end of the garden, we found ourselves facing the fence that marked the boundaries of the orphanage. The attendant, a thin man with delicate features and without a trace of a beard, motioned for us to follow him, helping us to slip through planks in the fence, some of which had been removed to allow us to get to school without going all the way around. We crossed the street with the attendant looking like a policeman or a mother duck standing in the middle of the street to make sure her fragile ducklings crossed over safely. Once we reached the school, the attendant called my sister and me and took us to the principal's office, full of carpets that were tired of faking a long-lost economic prosperity and exhausted from covering the time-worn walls. From there, we were shown to our classroom. Although my sister was older, they enrolled us in the same year. Probably because up until that point we hadn't received any formal education yet. Mishka was with us too. I felt calmer, I sat down between him and Alyona.

I was captivated by the dark green color of the benches. A worn scribbled-over green that continued to hold on. The teacher introduced herself: she was a beautiful woman, very young, blond, and she wore rather small, light blue, metal-coated glasses. They gave her an air of importance. If my sister and I knew how to write, it was only thanks to Babushka.

And it was also thanks to her that we had some skills in math, basic ones, but still a good start. Right away I realized that Mishka was an excellent student and the one to whom our teacher compared us. He was very good at reading aloud; he knew how to modulate his tone to highlight the important words. The first two hours of grammar were tedious. Then we did two hours of math in which I felt at ease: I was able to solve many problems and I received compliments from the teacher; I felt a sweet warmth on my cheeks, which for a moment seemed to heal the pain in my chest and ribs from the punches of the previous day.

At a certain point the bell rang and the hallway turned into a riverbed that was suddenly flooded with water: there were children everywhere, it seemed that they were coming out of the walls and running toward the exit, toward the finish lines of life, toward the freedom offered by knowledge. I hated school. We went back to the institute, left our backpacks in the rooms, and went to eat. The meal was good. I was afraid of Ivan and Arthur but there was no longer any reason for this feeling. Sergej explained to me that what had happened was a closed chapter. It was a ritual and the fact that I had not informed the attendants guaranteed me a peaceful coexistence from that point on. This silence was the form of respect that the older kids demanded. At the end of the meal, I took another green apple from the fruit counter. I said goodbye to my sister and headed up to my room. I climbed the steps three at a time, I wanted to get there before the others.

The room was enveloped in the soft warmth of autumn sunlight that refreshed the lackluster walls. I went to the window.

I decided to open it a little, just to let in some fresh air and disperse the stagnant smell. I took out the green apple I had put in my backpack at breakfast. I placed it by the window and, setting a foot on the bedside table, boosted myself up to sit on the windowsill. In my hand I had the green apple from lunch and began to eat it. The other, the one I had taken at breakfast, was there next to me enjoying the peace, the silence. It was my way—a ritual—for recalling my mother's memory. I made an agreement with myself: I would no longer associate the bag of apples that she had brought me on her last visit with anything unpleasant, but only with her spirit. Children have a great imagination, and I was doing fairly well with mine. The green apple allowed me to imagine her right there next to me. It didn't matter if contact between us wasn't possible, the idea of her safe with me in that room made me feel good. Remembering this scene now that I am an adult, I believe that I somehow repaired the world with this gesture. I had the feeling that the world was good: everything was possible again; perhaps she had left, but she had not gone away. The universe has many windows, and now Irina deserved a new view.

I have a strange relationship with windows. From an early age, they have always fascinated me. They are fixed within their frames; they don't have a hard life; on the contrary, they withstand the cold and in summer enjoy the sun. They have first-row tickets for viewing the world. And I have always wanted to see the world. Windows, for me, were the perfect means. As a child, I had negative experiences in the city but it still fascinated me, so I decided to observe life from inside the house. On those rare occasions when we were together with our mother, I kept my face at the window to observe the chaos that for me was life. I was convinced that all those people were driving their cars to an amusement park or a public square to see something special. And no, I didn't envy them. I knew there was some reason I wasn't able to go out myself but I was happy for them. I would often start yelling at those colorful but unresponsive cars: "Go at full speed! Drive around as much as you can! Come on! The park is about to close! Hurry!" I have always been happy for others who manage to be happy.

The apple was enjoying its peace next to me. After a few minutes, Sergej, Mishka, and Sasha arrived and started laughing. They told me that I looked like a crazy person, and I started laughing too, because maybe I was a little bit crazy. They asked me why the apple was there. And, from that moment on, we started sharing our experiences, knowing for a fact that we would be friends for life. I said I wanted to tell my story last because I wasn't used to talking about myself. We unpacked our still brief lives that had already tasted bitterness. Mishka started. He was a good-looking kid with a really pleasant voice. He looked like he belonged in a commercial. Big, light blue eyes stood out in contrast with his dark skin; he had a very small, elegant nose and a delicate chin. His bobbed hair gave him an air of spontaneity. No matter what he said, we would listen. He focused his gaze on the ceiling, letting his memories take over, and started talking about how he had lost his mom, and how a year later his dad also died from an undiagnosed illness. Mishka thought the pain of losing his wife had killed his dad. He told us how beautiful his life had been until his mother's death. She always read him a fairy tale to put him to sleep and, at breakfast, would carefully prepare a *chay* infused with the warmth of her heart. His big blue eyes turned red, and Mishka understood that it was time to stop. We kept quiet for a few seconds. I don't know how to explain that pause; it was a mix of sorrow and also respect for the courage he had demonstrated by sharing: we were all united by the loss of something important. Such a precocious loss that, when it struck, we didn't completely understand it. But wait, what was I saying? You never really understand that you have lost someone. For a few years you even remember their voice: you imagine that the person you lost is still there even without the slightest movement of air in your room. When you walk through the streets feeling miserable and think *I have to snap out of it*, you have the sense that the hand of the person you loved is caressing that thought. Sometimes, you even hear words accompanied by the voice of the person you know took care of you, raised you, made you laugh. Death is only the end of the physical experience; memories instead are proof that the person's warmth has no end.

It was Sasha's turn now. His face turned pink, he looked like a cherry ready to say goodbye to the season in which the sun had lovingly ripened it; his voice was heavy like the lowest key of a piano. He almost felt guilty saying that only his dad was dead and that his mother came by often to visit him. He was in an orphanage because his mother couldn't support him and his education. He said no more. Sergej coughed twice and started speaking with a dark angry tone. His short hair seemed to emit electricity that spread over his strange forehead, wide over a small head. He had icy eyes, an awkward mouth, wide teeth. He started by mentioning the mother he had never met; he thought he had seen her in a photo, but he found out that the photo was just an advertisement and that the woman portrayed in it was not his mother, but a model. What he said about his father I cannot repeat: I learned many obscene words on that occasion. His eyes weren't sad; they were angry. Full of an anger that you rarely see on such a young face; he looked like the devil incarnate. The anger he felt talking about his father assaulted me, too. It was the first and only time that I allowed the thought of my own father to cross my mind. I have never met him. I think this is quite telling, right? A father, alive and well, who does nothing to meet his son: I think this makes clear what a stretch it is to define someone like him with the term "man." All the times I was scared, or someone hit my mother in front of me, or I cried because Irina was gone, I never thought of him. I couldn't even imagine him at death's door. For me he has always been like a bee that lands on a flower, pollinates it, and flies away. That flower was my mother, who tried to bloom, in vain, but she will always live on in my memory. He, on the other hand, will neither live nor die in my memories because he never existed.

The four of us wanted to ask the director for permission to stay in the same room. We went downstairs, while the cooks were leaving the cafeteria to enjoy a cigarette. Walking through the hallway with my friends, I felt unstoppable. The noise of our footsteps was all that mattered. We had the feeling that although life had been bitter, we were invincible because we were not alone. Four boys with a shared experience of pain who were ready to support one another forever. We went into the director's office. There was a large succulent plant under the window, an apparently valuable wooden desk, a good fresh smell as if spring had settled there, and a black leather lounge chair. The sunlight caressed the furniture, lighting up the room and promising to return the next day. We sat on the plastic chairs next to the wall. A few seconds later the director stepped in. As always, his smile seemed to precede his arrival and gave us a sense of comfort. Mishka delivered our proposal and the director agreed to it. It was the best news of the day. The director was very happy about our enthusiasm, explaining the importance of friendship. He urged us to remain united, even when there were conflicts, because only through disputes do people grow. We stood up to leave, but the director stopped me and asked me to stay. I was worried; Mishka and Sergej looked at each other confused while Sasha didn't seem to notice anything. It was just a fraction of a second but I felt better when Mishka and Sergej looked at me as if to say, "Everything will be fine, stay calm."

The director stood up, and, now that it was just the two of us in the room, he asked: "Have you ever sat on a leather chair?" I said no, and so he asked me to try his. I didn't hesitate. I was happy and felt important. In that moment I forgot my loneliness. A few seconds later, though, I started wondering why he had asked me to stay. Taking some books from his bookshelf, he approached me. He put the books on the table, took a seat, and started talking. "So Kola, how are you? Do you like it here?" I replied: "Yes, sir." He laughed but then said with a serious tone: "You don't have to call me 'sir.' I am one of your friends." I was embarrassed. For me it was strange to hear an adult say something like that. I actually feared adults, especially men. I think this is because of my mom's brother. But I was also afraid of my maternal grandmother. They both lived in an orange building in a different neighborhood from Irina's, not that there was much of a difference. They lived on the third floor; a large door led to three apartments with a shared bathroom and a kitchen. From the time I was little, I have never really felt like I would retain fond memories of Irina's mother. She was an ugly woman with short hair, she always smelled of garlic and alcohol, and she screamed all the time. Once, when her partner died, to punish me she locked me in the room where the coffin lay open, waiting for the funeral. I didn't yet know people could die but I was terrified by the purplish color of his body. I screamed and kicked the door, but she laughed along with my uncle. My mother's brother was a blond young man, who, I think, escaped mandatory military service. He was muscular with broad shoulders. He was a pervert. The nights I slept in that house, I slept in his room. Every time he had a different girl, and every time, after satisfying himself, he would physically hurt her.

Even though I was scared, I felt happy in the director's office. That afternoon, the most beautiful thing possible happened: the director explained to me the importance of books.

Of course, lazy and ignorant as I was back then, I didn't immediately grasp the meaning of that moment, but over the years, I have come to appreciate it. He picked up a book and told me we reap so much from time spent reading. He said if we do nothing and just lie on the couch, our minds and souls gain nothing from the passage of time. But if we make use of our time reading, we live twice as long. He held a novel in his hand, which I know very well now: *The Idiot* by Dostoyevsky. A book I eventually read fourteen years later. I loved listening to him speak, it felt like he knew everything; life looked easy through his eyes. All of a sudden, he looked at me like a father and said: "You know, my name is Nikolai Nikolajevich and, when you grow up, you too will have this name!" I didn't understand and so he explained it to me. In Russia it is common to give children the same names as their parents. And when the children grow up, their name contains, in part, that of the parent plus a suffix. In my case, the one who had been responsible for my conception had my name: Nikolai. Kola is short for Nikolai. At first, I was upset. I thought it was a cruel twist of fate. I would forever carry the name of an individual I did not know and for whom I had no feelings. But the director's smile was contagious, and I understood that I too would be called Nikolai Nikolajevich like him, and not like the man who had abandoned my mother. I was happy. "You know, between the gate and the institute there is a small cabin. I shouldn't be telling you this, but if you climb to the roof of this cabin, you can see the apple orchard. I saw you today as I was walking down the hall. I noticed the care with which you placed the apple on the window, and I know what it means. I too once lost a very important person, and, like you, I am always looking for her in one way or another. I'll tell you a secret, but only because we have the same name: she is in all the pages of every book I have ever read or will read." I still remember those powerful words. It was the first time I saw a man demonstrate boundless love for a woman. It was proof that men can love women.

The director's words sounded like sweet music expressing the strength of a feeling that goes beyond physical experience. It was as if I was learning that, once you have given your heart to a person, you could love them just by finding them again in memories, or even in a smell that evoked their presence. It was a good feeling, I realized that I would never forget Irina.

Conversations between adults and children often just end in silence; but this time, the director kept talking, telling me to go get my things from my—now old—room and to move everything into Sergej and Mishka's room. In order to get to the upstairs floor, I had to cross the hall. That silent corridor, sometimes gloomy because of poor lighting, now seemed so friendly, and the fish in the aquarium seemed to gasp for breath more cheerfully, in small spurts, as if they were playing with the bronze ship resting on the bottom: they no longer missed the open seas as much as before. In a day that was not yet over, I was moved by small poignant occurrences that filled my soul with serenity and a dash of euphoria. I walked up the same old stairs quickly and went to get my stuff. I stepped into the room that I was about to leave and found Arthur reading a note. Upon seeing me, he blushed. I didn't ask anything. I had already understood how important my silence was in the presence of older kids. He addressed me first, thoughtfully, with a voice that seemed stolen from the sweetest kid in the world: "Kola, regarding yesterday, forget about it, we didn't mean to hurt you, the situation got out of hand. I'm sorry that Ivan punched you in the chest, but you know . . ." He didn't need to finish the sentence, it was all clear: everyone should know their place, and Arthur had acted accordingly. He continued talking: "As for what I said about your mother, I'm sorry. I don't really think that. I'm sure she's a fine woman. It's only because mine was a whore, and so in every mother I see her face." I remained silent, after all I was too young to tell right from wrong: What could a seven-year-old kid like me know about why my mother had led the life she did? I smiled. I picked up my stuff, and then Arthur spoke again: "Kola! The apple! You forgot the apple on the window!" I grabbed it, put it in my bag, and looked at Arthur clenching that white note in his hands, his face getting redder and redder. And I said to him: "If you want, I'll take it to her." I was very close to seeing lava pour out of his nostrils. He was like a volcano bubbling over with excitement, shame, and an inability to fake strength and toughness. He gave me the note, pointing out the room and bed to me. He didn't say anything, but he understood, I'm sure, that I would never tell anyone about it. Not because I was scared he would beat me up, but simply because I understood that, for him, it was only important that his words be heard by the person he intended.

As I said goodbye, he got into bed with his black Walkman headphones on. I went to my new room and put my things away. I didn't have to ask which bed to pick: they had left me the one under the window. I felt happy once again. I ran off to drop the note. I had to cross over to the girls' section, but it was really easy to go unnoticed: most of the girls were out in the little garden.

———

After completing my errand and skipping the optional snack, I went outside. Instead of going to the garden, I went to the cabin the director had mentioned. The sun was almost ready to give way to the moon and stars, but there was still a tiny glimmer of light. The air was cool, but that remaining ray of sunshine was strong enough to warm my face. The noise of the boys shouting and chasing each other in the garden accompanied my explorations. The cabin was very low to the ground, it looked like the lair of a good witch. It had a gabled roof that dominated the rest of the structure; its aqua green paint was now on the verge of rust. I was curious to see the apple orchard. So, I decided to climb. It was easy, the roof was really low: a more imaginative person would have pictured a secret military base inside extending underground. Once I was on top, a large orchard appeared. It was heavenly to my eyes: it seemed that the little sunlight left was waiting to give me time to gaze at the landscape. In the foreground there were the apple trees, apples of all colors: mostly red and green, but also some yellow ones. Looking out toward the horizon, one could feel a sense of peace. The light dissolved the contrast between the old houses and the apple orchard without melancholy. A crumbling road, worn out by time and neglect, was the only boundary between the two worlds. Birds in flight, cats lounging on top of gates, dogs barking, all so far off they seemed to be on the other side of the world, made me realize that beauty is hidden in the details. If it hadn't been for the apples, that view would have left me unmoved. But with the apples and the idea of Irina out there somewhere, even the rundown houses and the narrow road seemed wonderful to me. In the distance, you could even see smoke rising from the factories, ready to escape, and leave that place forever.

As I remember this moment, the cypress tree that shades my window from the sun bends intermittently with the wind, and soft flashes of light land on my desk and face, reproducing on my skin the same emotion I felt that day on the roof of the cabin.

I looked at the sky that was about to light up the first stars and went back inside.

There was still an hour until dinner, so I decided to explore the workshops on the ground floor. I went into the woodshop and found some kids I didn't know, along with the carpenter. He was a funny-looking man: thin, with sparse white hair and wrinkled skin like an early ancestor of the elephant. He smiled, showing me his few teeth, and asked my name. I introduced myself. The carpenter told me to try making a doorknob. After giving me safety glasses and light cloth gloves lined with rubber, he turned on the lathe, which made the wood turn, and told me to grab a chisel and to follow his moves. "Look how I do it. You have to bring the chisel close; when you feel contact with the wood, then you can press. You have to create a sort of ball. Do you understand what I mean? Kola, do you understand?" I nodded. When it was my turn, I asked the carpenter if he could help me. He started guiding my hands, shouting: "You see, Kola? We are making a wooden ball! See? You know how! Like that! Good job! Now you're on your own, I'm not guiding you. You can do it, press on the edge here and there!" I smiled, I was capable of making something. I had made a wooden ball. When it was ready, the carpenter turned the machine off; he took the chisel out of my hand and gave me another tool to smooth the edges of the sphere until it became a knob. He explained how to do it, and I followed his instructions to the letter. The knob was done! You just had to rub sandpaper against it to make it smooth. The carpenter enrolled me in his woodshop, explaining that there was no obligation, that enrollment was just a bureaucratic matter. I didn't go back to my room because it was already time for dinner. I met up with the other kids to eat together. Afterward, we went up to the room, and Sergej started playing the harmonica. He said he had found it among his aunt's things and had stolen it from her. He didn't know how to play it at all, but we had a lot of fun. We all gave it a try and took turns making fun of one another.

"Before one of you three leaves the orphanage, I'll play it like a god," smiled Sergej.

My new room was next to the previous one, where there were now two other boys, besides Arthur and Ivan. The commotion we created irritated Ivan, who came in and asked whose harmonica it was and took it away. He said he was going to piss inside it, so no one would try to play it again. We laughed at how he said this, and then he called in his roommates, including Arthur, to teach us a lesson. Ivan came toward me, but this time I stood up on the bed. I was ready to defend myself. Sergej did the same, then Mishka, and finally Sasha. We were four against four, even though the fight wasn't equally matched. Ivan reached out to hit me, but lost his balance. And I had the opportunity of a lifetime. Having never thrown a punch, I slapped him instead on his right ear. He let out an earth-shattering scream, yelling that he couldn't hear and that if he had lost his hearing, he would kill me. I wasn't scared, or maybe I was, but I couldn't look like a coward after having challenged him. As they threatened revenge, Arthur and the others left. They returned late at night: we were all sound asleep when they started beating us up and spitting on us. The lesson was delivered, and it hurt.

And that's how this most intense day in the new orphanage ended. It was new in some ways, but old in others.

~

One Sunday morning we woke up to snowflakes gently falling on the windowpanes. The sense of lightness we had all awaited was hidden in those small crystals. Watching the first snowfall of the season helped empty our minds, calming them. Whiteness seemed to cleanse our memories, sweeping away the worst ones. Everyone was moved by that beautiful scene, all the kids and even the director, who came up to our floor and started humming a song he made up on the spot. He walked into each room, sharing words of excitement.

It was difficult to remain indifferent to the dance of nature that was now changing all at once. It didn't matter if the snow was hiding the greenery on most days; each time it snowed, the falling flakes brought new sensations. Even the sky seemed to become clearer, abandoning its melancholy to make space for an inexplicably sweet nostalgia.

That first snowfall brought with it another joy for me to experience. The following Saturday I was to spend two days with Babushka Faya, and my heart was floating like a light balloon.

The week went by as fast as a cigarette burning in the wind, and finally that long-awaited Saturday arrived. I was already showing signs of euphoria early in the morning: I was smiling, joking, and couldn't sit still. The hours went by quickly, and finally Babushka arrived. The director welcomed her and asked an attendant to get me and my sister. We raced down the stairs as if we were flying. We ran into the room and hugged Faya without any formalities. My embrace lasted a few moments longer. Her smell enveloped me: mothballs, clean but old-smelling clothes, and a drop of perfume helped me understand that my happiness was real and that the week had passed quickly; the wait had not been in vain.

The director had her sign a form and said goodbye to us. We were allowed to spend two days with our Babushka. It is bizarre how a single signature is able to unfurl the sails of the heart: in that moment I was convinced that the pen Faya used was magical. We crossed the garden, now covered in snow, with steps as light as our thoughts. It was like walking on clouds. We took the bus, I think it was the 85 bus, and we headed toward Faya's neighborhood. Sitting down on the hard seats, I started observing the people around us. It was the daily life of others that I didn't usually have a chance to experience. There were many faces: young and more seasoned, smooth and worn, serene and worried. There was a pregnant woman smoking half a cigarette by a slightly open window. At every stop someone got off, but each face was promptly replaced by that of a new passenger. Sometimes you could hear the noise of the ticket machine. I saw a man arguing with a woman who had a black eye: he was apologizing but she wasn't having any of it. I didn't enjoy that scene at all.

We finally got off. Faya stepped between us and took us by the hand. Her palms were firm and warm but chapped and red from the cold. She walked us across the street with the attention of a woman hardened by experience. She then let go of our hands and told us not to leave her side. We had to take a long and narrow alley that Alyona and I knew by heart. There were a few old and badly parked cars and some tall trees that sheltered the asphalt from the snow; in fact, there was no whiteness but only some patches of ice. The buildings were the usual tall and gray, with dilapidated balconies that were sad from always facing such an unappealing view. Homeless people were parked on the benches. There was an acrid smell, a mixture of alcohol, vomit, and wet rags. After a few minutes, we reached Faya's building. It looked like so many others, with a discolored wooden door. Once inside, we took the elevator to the top floor. Faya smiled at me and told me to stay calm. I was afraid of elevators. Standing there, suspended inside that mechanical box, without feeling firm ground beneath me, reminded me of the instability of my life. I was always at the mercy of others, and the idea of not being in control made me nervous.

Once we reached the ninth floor, we went into the apartment.

Every little detail of that place is imprinted in my memory. Even now, I can still savor the taste of that apartment as I write and light up yet another cigarette to feel the warmth of those colors again.

The door was large, of heavy iron; once opened, there was a small corridor. On the right you could see the bathroom, next to it was the kitchen, very small but cozy. It faced the balcony along with the now empty bedroom of Babushka's brother, who was taken away from us by alcoholism. Faya's long narrow room looked out onto the same balcony. Upon entering, there was a piece of furniture that covered the entire wall. The left side served as a closet, and on the other side there was a cupboard filled with glasses. A TV was wedged in between. On the opposite wall, there was Faya's very tall, full-size bed as well as the sofa bed where my sister and I slept. The apartment was small, but very bright. Only the small corridor, with an old nightstand and large mirror, was swallowed up by darkness. I always assumed the mirror was a gift, as it was out of place: too flashy for such humble surroundings.

The smell of the place clung to Faya's clothes, and since she was a very good person, it was, for me, the scent of goodness. The smell was neither clean nor fresh, but a scent of life. Of a woman whose face was marked by the years, who lived humbly, with a job that enabled her to support herself and be always busy. She carried on, without expectations. She worked at a train station: when she worked the night shift she slept there, in a small room with a bed and a tiny blue kitchen. Alyona and I once stayed in that place, too. It was fun to watch Babushka direct the train traffic, and the sound of the railcars was pleasant. It was never clear to me what her role was, but she had a job that gave her dignity. A dignity that was often trampled on in those neighborhoods. I like to think that she fought to have that job, that she studied and attended courses and rejected the idea of being eaten up by a sad fate. She was about sixty years old, with shortish gray hair, almost white, and when she went out to do chores she would cover it under a silk headscarf. It fit her perfectly: she seemed the most settled and confident lady in the world. She had hazel eyes, small and nicely shaped, with very pronounced crow's-feet. I wouldn't be lying if I said that, when she was young, she was a beautiful woman. Her nose was soft and regular, and she had thin lips above which you could see, against the light, a soft grayish mustache. She was sturdy, with heavy hands and ungainly legs. In winter she wore either a blue or an orange jacket. Her closet was small and everything inside absorbed the smell of mothballs. It was really nice to spend time with her. She was very serious, thoughtful, and determined. From that moment on, we would spend every weekend there. Each Saturday, as soon as we got to her place, we would take a nice hot bath. She would give us clean clothes, so she could wash ours. In the evening, we often ate borscht, and by nine we were already in bed. Before we fell asleep, we watched the children's channel on TV. At that time, there was a cartoon in which the animals and the stars spoke and communicated with each other. At the end of the episode, the moon sang a good-night song. I never found out how it ended, I always fell asleep during the first few notes. Babushka often read us fairy tales; she explained them to us, trying to teach us something. Of all the weekends we went to her place, I remember two in particular. One, when Alyona and I were chasing each other around the room and I hurt myself under the eye, leaving a scar that is still somewhat visible on my face. The other weekend I remember was when I found my first toy. I was looking at the sky from the balcony, when all of a sudden, looking down, I noticed a small gray spot. Curious, I went downstairs to see, and when I realized it was a very large toy car, I was so happy. I shouted with amazement. I took it to Babushka's apartment, and I didn't care that it only had three wheels. It was mine! I played with it for the rest of the day. I wanted to take it to the orphanage, but Faya advised me to leave it at her place because the older kids were likely to steal it.

On Sunday mornings we would walk around the city and sometimes went to church. I was happy those times we went to Mass. Not so much for the religious part as for the candle I used to light in memory of Irina after leaving a one-ruble donation. Other times we would go eat cotton candy, or visit the street markets. In the evening we would take a bus back home. There would be another hot bath and another hot meal. Then Faya would help us pack, adding candies and chocolates to our backpacks. We would listen to the good-night song and fall asleep. Serenely.

My weekends were all pretty similar. Since Babushka was elderly, we only did simple things. But it didn't matter: the main thing was that she spent time with us. I always wondered why a woman like Faya didn't have a partner. She deserved one; indeed, any man would have been lucky to be with her. Babushka is constantly in my thoughts, I think about her all the time. Now and then, I picture her sweet face, marked by the wrinkles that time deposited over the years, holding within themselves the traces of memories. I would love to be one of those wrinkles, to caress her face and remind her that I'm there, that I have never forgotten her, and that I'm grateful to her and always will be. If I feel compassion, tenderness, and the desire to do something for someone I don't know, it's because she, though a distant relative, took care of us. It's as if she had smoothed out our stay in Russia with thoughtfulness and care: even if she didn't erase the pain, she brightened our days.

~

Weekends with Babushka were always too short, just long enough to ease our hearts. Leaving the orphanage meant watching the world pass before our eyes, which were like windows removed from the lives of others. It was like reaching out to try to grab something and ending up with an empty fist. Even so, it was nice, it was nice to watch the world. I often had the feeling that people out there didn't realize they existed. They had who knows how many possibilities, but they just stood there like low-lying plants, indifferent to life's winds, waiting for the end. While my friends and I, locked up in that orphanage, never missed an opportunity to breathe in the excitement of life, even if only for a moment, imagining we had a great future ahead of us. Of course, later, it wouldn't take much to bring us down to earth again, wondering if we would ever belong to the world out there. The days went by quickly, more or less all the same. The stagnant air of the hallways was occasionally moved by the visit of social workers. They came in old cars, almost always Ladas, the most popular cars in Russia at that time. We could see them from the windows, as the director welcomed them. They always left without coming up to the second floor, where we spent the rest of our day after school. However, we all knew they would be back soon, and not alone, but with couples ready to rewrite their lives by adopting a child. The only one who was indifferent to the presence of these couples was Ivan, aware that he was too old to be adopted. This enraged him. I think he felt a deep despair, as he became more and more certain that he would have to get ready to fight for his life all alone. Once some Americans came. They came with a big car, bringing many gifts for all the children. It turned out that they were there for Maria, a thirteen-year-old girl. I remember her hair, excessively blond, her thin face and her hollow eyes. She had an irritating, very high-pitched voice. She always wore a red sweater that dulled her already pale complexion. On her right cheek, she had a conspicuous mole, and she was teased a lot because of it. I never thought much about her. For me she was just a nameless face who didn't show any emotion, except in those days, when she was the center of attention. She was called into the visiting room and from there she emerged with a contagious smile that showed all her teeth, especially the two canines, disproportionately large compared to her incisors. She looked like a vampire. She was wearing a gold necklace: the sparkle attracted Ivan's attention. So, after Maria showed off her happiest expression, almost to humiliate us, the director, knowing how things worked, advised her to give back the necklace and to retrieve it when it was time to leave for America. I remember she was adopted after a short time. The farewell day was a celebration. She was so happy that she left each of us a chocolate bar, telling us that soon the opportunity to leave the orphanage would come for us, too. As she said goodbye to her friends, she started to cry and an attendant choked up. The director shook her new father's hand firmly: that handshake was intense. I have never forgotten the details: I watched the director's gaze fall on Maria's father's face and in that moment time stood still, I'm sure. It was the director who released the grip, as if, before withdrawing his hand, he had ascertained the seriousness and commitment of the new father.

The supper following Maria's departure was silent; we were told that another couple would come the next day. We were curious, thrilled but scared. Whose turn would it be? Ivan joked that it would be his turn, that he was the oldest, and that if they didn't take him to the visiting room, he would beat up anyone who went in.

That afternoon arrived fast, and we were all looking out the windows. A beautiful, burgundy Rolls-Royce drove through the gate. And right then, each of us expressed the same wish: "Let me be the one to get into that car!" Four people, two men and two women, got out of the car and disappeared through the entrance door. We were frantic. Mishka told me it was my turn; I smiled and replied that it was easier for a single child to be adopted rather than two. That instant, the attendant knocked at our door: "Kola, come with me!" My heart pounded, my hands were numb, I felt like a cloud hit by lightning. I followed her in silence. As we made our way to the visiting room, it was odd not to see my sister in the hall. I thought that maybe she was already inside. The attendant knocked, and I felt like someone was about to open the doors to my future. I stepped into the room and was immediately struck by my sister's absence. I noticed the elegant curtains covering the windows, the walls decorated with gold and black tapestries. There was a stereo in the lower right corner. In the middle of the room, there were two sofas, one in front of the other. On the sofa facing away from the window a couple was sitting. The man was thin, with blond hair except for the first gray strands on his neck, and with cold light eyes. My eyes immediately shifted over to the woman. She had light eyes too, but they were very small, surrounded by deep wrinkles, like those of a funny little mouse. She had a pronounced double chin, despite her thinness. Many freckles dotted her face, which would have otherwise been colorless. I sat on the sofa in front of them. There was a social worker, a shortish woman with excessive makeup. In trying to hide her age, she looked older than she was. And there was also the translator. He had a pleasant face, with a very large crooked nose, light brown eyes, and an untended beard. The husband started speaking in a language I didn't know; I later found out that those were the first English words my ears had ever heard. I felt detached from the scene with my legs crossed and my hands nervously playing with each other. The translator told me that I was a beautiful child and that I looked like the lady's grandfather. I didn't say a word. They kept talking to me but I was already somewhere else; I wished I were in my room. Suddenly I blurted out: "Where's my sister?" Silence fell, and embarrassment filled the whole room. No one knew what to say, so I insisted again: "Why isn't Alyona here with me?" This time the man, touching his forehead and nose, turned to the translator and spoke to him. The translator raised his head and looked at me: "Well, Alyona is not here because this kind couple is only interested in your profile." Those words shattered me, and in a matter of seconds, I was no longer myself. I began to smell the perfume of those two people: very nice, but too much for me. I noticed the gold ring on the woman's finger, it seemed expensive: too much for me. They kept talking, and the translator struggled to keep up with the pace of the conversation. They told me about their professions: he was a successful entrepreneur, she was a university professor. They wanted to take me to England, to a large house, with a swimming pool and a green lawn. I would have all the toys I could imagine. They would love me, as if they were my birth parents. But it seemed to me that they were buying me: I would be separated from Alyona in exchange for that beautiful future. In return for their offer, I could only repay them with the loneliness created by the separation from my sister. And I shouted: "I don't want to go with you without Alyona!" They took no notice of my words, saying I would understand when I was older. So, with watery eyes, I asked if they had any siblings, and they said no. Of course, I told them, they couldn't understand what I was saying, since they had no siblings. Again, they ignored my words. Children have little say in these matters, but in the orphanage, everyone knows what to do to discourage an unwelcome couple. And so, I changed my expression, I stood up and started yelling things I don't even remember anymore.

They got scared, and since, when playing a part, if you want to be believable you have to play it to the max, I started pulling my hair out. The pain made me scream even more. Others, hearing my screams, started chanting together: "Kola! Kola! Keep yelling! Kola! Kola!" That collective cry numbed the pain; I was sure that I'd go crazy for real if they adopted me without Alyona, and I continued until the director arrived. He looked at me, then he rested his eyes on the social worker: "How much hair does he still have to pull out before they leave? Do you even know how to do your job? Don't you think Kola has sufficiently demonstrated his complete lack of interest? And also, excuse me, where is his sister?" The woman stammered out some words, explaining how she was told that it was possible to adopt me alone. The director reddened, held his breath, and used all his patience and years in the field to diplomatically respond: "There's been a mistake here, I was not told that only Kola would meet this couple! Even just now in my office, we talked about the entire file, and that file contains both siblings!" The social worker didn't know what to say: she held on to the fact that permission had been given to her from the higher-ups. This time the director did not hold back: "Instructions from the higher-ups? And tell me, these people who gave you instructions, have they ever been in an orphanage? Have they ever seen sadness and fear on children's faces? Do they know what it's like to feel lonely, to be all alone? If you take Alyona away from Kola, he will go crazy; she's all he has. It is not possible to adopt him without her; I'm the one who objects! And please don't take any more adoption cases in this institute. You are a social worker, but only by title, not because you have any sense!"

I was stunned, no one had ever defended me like this. The social worker didn't say a word and then left the room, slamming the door. As she crossed the hall, the kids mocked her. The couple did not ask the translator anything. Before leaving the room, they gave me a one-hundred-dollar bill, but the director admonished them: "Folks, this is not what children need! It's best if you just go now, otherwise I will flag your profile with the authorities, and they will bar you from adopting on Russian soil!" The two understood and left. The translator apologized to the director for the distress created by the situation, patted me, and before disappearing behind the door, said: "You are tough. I can tell you have a little sister. I have one too, her name is Paulina."

~

What happened in the visiting room really upset me. In the nights that followed, I dreamed those people were taking me away. It was a nightmare, because Alyona was never present. I began to fear losing what little I had left. It's not as if my sister and I had a close relationship or anything; she was always with the girls. But I knew we were destined to be really happy together, or I was even more certain that if we were separated, it would become pointless for either of us to seek happiness. I was a kite and she was the wind. Without Alyona I would remain on the ground and never take off. I didn't want to lose her. But that visit had made me aware of a reality that often escapes children: our separation was possible. I wondered, in the silence of my room and the hallways, why the possible scenarios affecting my fate were all unwelcome. I began to think a lot, and in a dark way. It was too early for such thoughts, I was only seven years old.

I didn't feel like being with my friends; I always felt the need to check that my sister was still there. During meals, I often lost my train of thought in conversation because I was frantically looking for her, or I would jump to my feet, to have a better view and make sure I could see the color of her hair at some table.

That tension brought on a collapse of my immune system and I came down with a high fever. One ordinary afternoon I was taken to the hospital. I remember a strong headache, a burning forehead, and losing my balance. An ambulance arrived; the director reassured me: he would come visit with my sister if I was gone for a long time. On the way to the hospital, the nurses had me lie down, started an IV in my left arm, and asked questions about my family's medical history. I didn't understand and had no idea what to say. I knew nothing about my family. Once we got to the hospital, I was placed on a stretcher and taken to a ward.

As they wheeled me through the neon-lit corridors, I could see the precariousness of that old structure: the ceiling and the walls were full of cracks and the air was dense with a really strong odor, which penetrated my chest and remained there the whole time of my hospital stay. The nurse in charge of taking me to a room on the third floor was friendly. She was plump with short, reddish hair and light eyes. Her teeth were yellow, and when she smiled she looked ten years older, but her laugh was engaging. She took care to reassure me, telling me it was just a fever and that she would take some blood samples for some routine tests. When we reached our destination, I finally got off the stretcher. I was in a large room together with other children. The obvious immediately struck my eyes and heart: they were all in the company of their mothers. Each bed had a cot beside it where the women could spend the night. I once again felt a sense of loneliness: the difference between me, my life, and that of others. I went over to the window to look out. Moving the dusty, cream-colored curtains aside and leaning out, I studied the view: it looked like the painting of an artist who had lost every sense and memory of peace. There was little to see. The wall of the building bordered a small road. There were no trees, no people, not even a bench. I would have preferred a window drawn on the wall or no window at all. I went back to my cot and all the mothers took turns figuring out what I had and asking about my family. They immediately realized that it was a painful topic and that it was better not to ask too many questions. I let the tears pour out, each tear expressing the anguish of that situation; no one was there with me and I feared never seeing Alyona again. Who knows, maybe they would take advantage of my absence to move my sister by convincing her that I would never come back. These thoughts tormented me. I got used to the company of the children and their mothers right away, even if seeing them take care of their children made me feel even more lonely. The nurses took me into their hearts. For every injection, if I didn't complain, they would give me a treat: candies or chocolates.

I also got used to the smell. There was a stench of alcohol and disinfectants hanging in the air that barely managed to hide the acrid and heavy odor of illness and suffering. In the rooms I entered—often, to cheer myself up and pass the time, I would join the nurses on their rounds—there was a stale smell of the relatives' worn and filthy clothes mixed with the smell of sweaty, old mattresses. Each room was more or less the same, some with extra beds, others with fewer: entering through a light metal door, there was, immediately to the right, a very small bathroom, with worn mirrors that were tired of being there and sad from having to reflect the image of illness instead of the beauty of life. Right past the bathroom, one could see that the iron beds were painted in a hurry. The whole room was lit by natural light, as the windows were very large. The walls were white with jaundiced tones, traces of time that seemed never to pass for some patients and, instead, flew by for others.

The rooms were also defined by the faces of the sick and of their loved ones. There were the tired but happy faces of those who were finally able to leave that place with the possibility of starting their lives again. There were those filled with fear and hope, a fear and hope that very slowly gave way to resignation. And when you met resignation in the eyes of the sick, the light coming from the windows seemed to disappear.

My hospitalization lasted three months. I never really found out what they treated: I didn't understand all those medical terms, and even if they explained them to me in the simplest way, I didn't have a mom to sweeten them with some story. The routine of those days slowed down time. They woke me at six to take my temperature, at eight there was breakfast for those who could have it and the first dose of medicine. At eleven, another round with the thermometer, and then a wait for lunch. I was lucky, I had no food restrictions. The best day was

Wednesday: for lunch they served soup with a chicken leg, and in the evening baked potatoes with fish.

Nights passed by quickly, with the shadow of the wall lamp in front of my bed keeping me company. When it was windy it felt like the silhouette disappeared, and I was afraid. Sometimes, I would cry before falling asleep, because, unlike my roommates, I had no one to tuck me in. Toward the end of December, that void was filled by a nurse: Katiusha. She was a beautiful woman with long black hair that she always kept tied up. Her face was pale but endowed with depth and intensity thanks to her gorgeous green eyes. When she laughed, dimples formed on her cheeks and her white teeth took over the scene. She had the gift of making you feel important; she loved her job. She was always kind, thoughtful, and never panicked. It felt like she was the one who had invented the profession of nursing; even older colleagues often respectfully sought her advice. I entered the hospital at the end of November 1997, and she noticed me around the Christmas season. During those weeks, patients' friends and relatives were coming and going. Nobody came to see me. Where was Babushka? Where were the director and Alyona? Had they forgotten about me? These were my thoughts. Katiusha noticed me. It was as if she had sensed my feeling of invisibility, even though I was clearly visible as I wandered the halls: I didn't feel like I was really there. So, on Christmas day she brought me a bag full of chocolates and a remote-controlled toy car. Seeing those gifts, and the smile with which she handed them to me, I burst into tears. Someone had noticed me, and it was someone who had nothing to do with my life: a wave of emotions came over me. For a moment, abandoning the stagnant grayness that had, at this point, taken possession of my senses, I could perceive all the colors in the world. I had no reason to envy the other children in my room. Forgotten by everyone, I too, surprisingly, had a person who was aware of my existence. Once again, my sense of loneliness took a break, before returning, as always, infinitely monotonous. The Christmas season was very beautiful. The mothers of the other children had also noticed that I never received visitors and took turns spending time with me. There was a lot of talk about dreams, and one woman said that children must always carry their dreams in their pockets. That same woman noticed that my pants and my shirt—the only clothes I possessed—had no pockets. So, a few days later she came with a gift in a sparkling bright green bag that she left for me at the foot of the bed. I peeked in, it was a pair of pants. Her smile, the motherly smile of a woman who knew how to be a mother, was the real gift that day.

My fever was almost always high, so I had to stay in bed most of the time. When it subsided, I would make the rounds with nurses and spend hours imagining myself skiing. The hallway was very long and narrow, barely the width of two beds. The floor was covered with a dark cream-colored lacquer. One day, while sitting outside the room playing with my toy car, I noticed that if I put all my body weight on my knees, I would slide. So I tested it out: sitting on my knees, with the help of my arms, I started to push. And there I was, sliding forward, and that's how those knees turned into a pair of skis, and those arms became ski poles diving into the snow. At first, all the staff thought I had gone crazy, but over time, the doctors and nurses, realizing that I had found a way to separate from my sadness, started participating in my game. Even the head physician, a very serious person everyone feared who rarely indulged in a belly laugh, went along with my fantasy. Whoever crossed my path started yelling: "And now Kola is about to complete the last kilometer of the race and he's all alone in the lead!" Every now and then, a nurse at the end of their shift would appear alongside me and start challenging me. And then, I would put all my energy into those little arms; I didn't want to lose. But, in fact, I always won! The nurse named Andrej would flash past me at the start and in a few seconds would be at least ten meters ahead. Then, seeing me look disheartened, he would start pretending all kinds of disasters were destroying his skis. One time he had to stop because he was being attacked by a bear (and his colleague started attacking him, pretending he was a real bear!). Another time, when we were about to start our race, he received an urgent call: "Oh no!" he said. "My skis have been eaten by beavers, I can't race, I'm going to have to buy new ones!" It was a lot of fun; over time I became the mascot of the hospital. The injections, the blood tests were now a habit, I didn't even feel the pain anymore.

Time went by and my fever came down. I spent more and more time with the nurses, and with Katiusha, who explained to me how a thermometer works and why the mercury moved from one degree to another. She told me about her wedding and how happy she was that day, but now she no longer knew how to convey the warmth of that happiness. She showed me pictures of her two girls, complaining that she wasn't able to spend enough time with them. She told me that I should choose a good job that would leave me time to spend with my family, a job that would enable me to change my life and forget the neighborhood I came from, and that money was useful, but that poor wretches like us would never be rich or free of the smell of old houses, even if we bought new ones. "You should get away from here to change your life and leave the past behind you." She was tired, like all people who live a life so different from what they had imagined. She was very pessimistic when she opened up, sometimes inconsistent. She was certain one had to rely on an honest job to get to the end of the month in peace, but without expecting to get ahead, because our dreams share the same foundations as houses in abandoned neighborhoods. Fragile houses, destined to collapse at the first tremor. Dreaming in those parts of town meant giving up, becoming sick with unattainable desires. When she spoke about these matters, her expression faded, her large eyes became small and stormy gray. She was scarred by a restlessness inside, maybe her choices had been dictated by a rush to grow up.

And even if, in that moment, among needles and medicines, I didn't realize how much I appreciated her, as I grew up, I understood she was one of those people who cross your path by chance and for only a short period, but with their gestures and words nurture your way of thinking and seeing things. I didn't know anything about her, aside from her brief reflections in the moment. Maybe she had a troubled childhood like mine, and yet at work she showed off her most beautiful smile, and you would never think she had faced dark times.

Shortly after Christmas, a distant aunt, whose name I can't remember, came by to visit me. I had seen her a few years back, during a holiday I spent in the countryside with my great-grandmother. Physically, she looked very Nordic: tall, with a stately build, light eyes and unruly blond hair. Her skin hung loose from her arms like butter left out in the sun, and if she started to wave them, you could see small waves dancing nervously. She was a woman of few words and knew how to make herself understood with a simple gesture. Her husband, Uncle Dimitri, was of average height, with a balding, sun-aged forehead. He wore small lopsided glasses, and when he laughed, you could see his right canine was missing. He smelled of alcohol but never got drunk, or so he believed. They were a beautiful couple, even from far away you could see how they complemented each other: he had a calm expression, almost distracted, while she was always looking around apprehensively. They had two children, Andrej and Helena. They were my only cousins, photocopies of their mother. We often played together during the holidays: we made slingshots and small flutes and raced on our bikes. Helena was already a young woman, familiar with boys. She never spoke to me or Alyona, as she was always in front of the mirror, in a hurry to become an adult. Our great-grandmother was the mother of Irina's father. She was very old, but still quite active. She was short and thin. The wrinkled skin of her face revealed all the years she had lived as a peasant. Her deep blue eyes, in comparison, were timeless. She always wore a red scarf on her head. She lived in the immense countryside with Georgi, the only son who had stayed nearby; I remember his olive complexion, which stood out in sharp contrast to his green eyes. Their little house was welcoming; they had built it with their own hands and took care of it obsessively. The first thing you saw was a plain fence that was always closed to keep the hens from escaping. A flimsy, sky-blue door was at the top of three cement steps covered with bright orange wood. The contrast between the light blue and dominating orange colors was striking. Stepping in, one encountered the smell of wood that had absorbed humidity and smoke from the fireplace: it reminded me a lot of the scent of incense in its most acrid form. Walking straight ahead, one arrived in the bedrooms, furnished with small cabinets and beds. The atmosphere was welcoming. If, after entering, you immediately turned right instead, you would find yourself in the kitchen, with tiled walls and a stone floor. There were some chairs around a wooden table and, on the other side of a curtain, a fireplace that functioned as a modern stove. Everything that landed on the table came from this large fireplace. It had a particular shape: a small opening, but not too small, just wide enough to contain medium-sized logs. Above the fireplace, there was a sort of loft and on the coldest nights we could sleep there, curled up in the rising heat. I'm still very attached to that little house. There was a garden in the back; you accessed it by opening a small door and passing through the shed where the goats and chickens slept. The garden was full of fruits and vegetables, according to the season. There were plenty of apple trees, one for each member of the family, even one for me and one for Alyona. But most importantly, there was Irina's tree: I must have spent whole days under that tree, eating only her apples. Irina was there with me, I'm sure. At the end of the summer season, it was time to harvest the potatoes. Alyona and I enjoyed picking the yellow and black beetles off the tubers. At the end of the day, we would dig a hole to gather and cover the potatoes before lighting a fire. When the fire died down, we would take the potatoes out and eat them. They had a smoky taste, like a good day at the end of summer. There was a magnificent blue sky at that time of the year. If I close my eyes today, I can still hear the hens nibbling on the seeds and see my uncle Georgi coming into the kitchen, his shoulders laden with the bucket of water he has drawn from the village well. I can smell the homemade bread and see the colors of sunset settle on nearby houses, creating soft tones that keep me company until I fall asleep. I see my sister returning home with a hedgehog, one of the few times I have seen her so happy. I remember my tears when the old rooster got knocked down, dethroned, by the younger one. I remember, smiling, how I discovered that the chicken broth I liked so much had been made with that same rooster for whom I had shed goodness knows how many tears. Another reason I have such sweet memories of that village and that little house is that it was there I discovered we get older every year and celebrate birthdays. Until I was six, I didn't know what a birthday was. I had just woken up on the morning of August 21, 1996, when my great-grandmother surprised me. She had prepared an important breakfast, fresh goat milk and a strawberry tart, and then she told me that in the evening we would celebrate my birthday. I didn't understand what she meant. Evening came and we were all at the table. In the afternoon, Uncle Dimitri had returned from a hunting trip with two ducks. That was his gift to me. Georgi gave me five rubles, which I could spend in the only shop in the village. He already knew what I was going to buy: *sgushchjonnoe molokò*—condensed milk—and chewing gum. My great-grandmother's gift was a wonderful cake she had made. It was a tart in the shape of the number 6, the age I had reached. I was so excited and wanted to eat it right away, but Andrej told me to wait, we had to add some candles. Once the candles were lit, with me and Alyona laughing at the fabulous surprise, they told me to blow them out after making a wish, and I did.

"I want to be happy like this my whole life."

I had touched happiness with my hand and I didn't want to let it go.

My aunt's visit to the hospital made me remember every detail of that place and that summer full of warmth.

Very detached, as always, she gave me a robotic hug and asked me how I was. I told her that I was much better now and that I was only twenty days away from leaving the hospital. She told me about Alyona, that she sent me warm greetings, and explained why Faya hadn't come to see me. She had been admitted to another hospital, they had to operate urgently, one hundred and fifty stitches in her abdomen. I started to cry, I wanted to go see her but it wasn't possible. To distract me, my aunt gave me a box of Legos. I was ecstatic, I had only seen

Legos on TV and I really wanted them. In addition to the Legos, she had brought me some chocolates. I ignored the toys to focus on the sweet taste of the chocolates. My aunt stayed another ten minutes and then left. It was a courtesy visit, I don't think she cared much about me, I only saw her in the summer and only because we were living under the same roof. Those twenty days passed by quickly. The hospital staff celebrated my recovered health and departure with joy. Everyone gave me a big hug. My roommates' mothers said goodbye and I made my way downstairs to wait for someone from the orphanage to come and pick me up. Katiusha stayed by my side until I left, nervously smoking two cigarettes. She told me she was happy that I had recovered but that at the same time she was sad because we would never see each other again. I promised I would come back and see her but she responded sternly: "People come here so they can leave and not come back. Many lead a hard life, but still, they want to get out. This is a hospital; you never want to be admitted, and if you are, you want to leave as soon as possible: it is the antechamber of death. I work here to make a living. I take care of others but it's just a job. If I had made the right choices, I would probably be teaching now. Here it's like a school, only you help people either to get well or to die, while in schools you help children live. They are similar but opposite places. I don't want to see you here again, and if this is the only place where we can meet, then I say to you: 'Do svidaniya! Farewell!' I look into your blue eyes and see a smile that disappeared too soon, and I feel anger. But I have seen you play, I have heard you talk, and I have seen you look out at the snippet of sky that can be glimpsed from the window: you have life in your eyes, now you think you have nothing, but soon enough you and your sister will have the opportunity to flourish. Everyone has this opportunity, even I had it, but I was too obsessed with my longing to run away from home. I have a mother, but it's not enough for a mother to bring you into the world; she has to believe in your potential; instead, my mother believed I was only capable of buying her cigarettes and alcohol. Let's make a deal: you grow up and don't come back here, and I quit smoking right this very minute! If I ever start smoking again, it will be because one evening, returning from work, tired, with my hands shaking from lack of sleep, I will feel a slight breeze, and this will be a sign from the heavens about you, about how you gave up. After all, if a kid gives up, maybe we should all give up, and I'll start smoking again, in the hope of seeing you here again and cursing you out for not making good use of your life!"

It was a deep and intense speech; at that point, I thought I had already grown up. She started to cry, I didn't know why, so I hugged her. That hug was interrupted by a familiar voice. "Kola! Here you are!" I turned around and it was the director, smiling. "You can't be left alone for a minute, you've already won over all the girls! And once you break these girls' hearts, don't try then to console them, otherwise they'll fall in love with you even more and they'll kill themselves for you!" Katiusha started laughing and the director's tone affected everyone in the lobby. He took my documents. Only at that point did I start to take my eyes off Katiusha, who, seeing me leave, threw the pack of cigarettes in the wastebasket and waved at me. I saw her disappear behind the door. Now, when I smoke, sometimes, it feels sweet to inhale, and this feeling brings me back to her and her words. It's a paradox: in remembering her, as the smoke enters my lungs, I feel like I am breathing better.

I stood still for a few moments, hoping to see her again at the door, but the director told me we had to go. We got into the car and drove back to the institute. All the kids were waiting for me in the cafeteria. My three friends hugged me and asked if I had been looking under the skirts of the nurses, and I answered, surprising myself: "No, not under the skirts, but I saw some people's hearts in their eyes!" They all started laughing, Sasha called me a faggot, and the director, hearing what I said, interrupted the commotion: "Kids, here's some cake and apple juice, let's make a toast to our Kola, who left with a 107-degree fever and came back a poet." The cheering drowned him out, until he yelled: "Wait, wait! When I went to get him, he was hugging a beautiful woman who was crying! Our Kola is a pro. Be careful, ladies, watch out for Kola!" Everyone burst out laughing, even Alyona smiled. Ten minutes of havoc followed and the director didn't step in; he actually participated in the party, telling jokes. He was a wonderful person, he knew what to say and how to say it at the right moment. I was happy to see those people again.

~

It was late March, the daily routine had kicked in again, snow continued to fall, and my terrible relationship with the school had not changed. Only in math did I get a five, the highest grade. My nights were peaceful; in some ways I had matured in the hospital. Week by week, we got to April, an incredible month: for fifteen days we celebrated the anniversary of the institute's creation. The city's politicians visited, we were given new clothes, we partied every evening with music and games in the main hall on the ground floor, a hall that I had never seen before. It was large, with wooden floors and huge windows. There was a piano and a large TV. Festivities took place there for fourteen days straight. On the first evening we had new clothes: I wore the pants that a mother from the hospital had given me in the little green bag. In my pocket I found a note that said:

> ALWAYS CARRY YOUR DREAMS WITH YOU, AND IF YOU THINK YOU WILL FORGET A DREAM, PUT

IT IN THIS POCKET. WEAR THESE PANTS WHEN YOU ARE LEAST HAPPY AND THEY WILL BRING YOU CLOSER TO YOUR DREAM.

I was very happy. In a short period of time, I had experienced some incredible things that had calmed me down. Those two weeks were intense. I discovered the effect of alcohol on us kids and on the director, who was always at the center of attention with his funny demeanor. We also received a van with sixteen seats as a gift. Now we could go swimming, because the town had also paid for our one-year membership to the pool.

With the end of the institute's festivities, my newfound calmness disappeared. I started sleeping poorly, not eating well, annoying those around me, and avoiding my roommates. I no longer looked for my sister in the dining room. Since I wasn't able to sleep at night, I slept in class at my desk besieged by nightmares, and often it wasn't the teacher who woke me up in a huff, but the sensation of drowning in my dream. I would pee in my pants. This situation worried my roommates first and then the attendants. When the director found out, he tried talking to me, but I was as silent as the grave in those days: I just sat there without a word, my only response came from my legs swaying back and forth. I was moved to the sickroom of the institute for two weeks. They would place a mask over my eyes and connect it to a machine that inscribed confusing and crooked lines onto a white piece of paper. "You have to be monitored" was the phrase they kept repeating in those days. But being in the dark was upsetting, and I was unable to relax: I couldn't breathe. Soon after falling asleep, I would wake up in a panic: I had to take off the mask, and when I did, I saw that white paper full of incomprehensible signs that perfectly reflected my confusion and distress. After two weeks, the director invited me to go with him, by car, to get some ice cream but then he said to me, "For your own good—because you need to sleep like all children your age, so that you can grow up nice and strong—you have to go stay for a few days in an institution with wacky but funny doctors," a psychiatric hospital. When he left me with the nurse, I started to cry. It was as if my best friend had betrayed me. I didn't understand. My tears were silent and looked like raindrops that the clouds had held back for a very long time. Now, as I write and the corner of my desk farthest from the window is covered by the shadow of the cypress tree, I remember that the hospital had a traditional facade of orange bricks. Inside, there were three very compact floors. I was assigned to the last room on the hallway, which overlooked a cemetery behind the building. There were no smells in that place, no outside noises, and the nurses were silent: I sensed something was off. I spent two weeks there. They did various tests on me with some very noisy machines. "Okay, we're done" were the technician's words. Cold as he was, with messy hair and those three missing teeth showing through his sad smile, I thought it was the right place for someone like him. But not for me. I don't want to become like him, I told myself. The strange thing is that I wasn't taking any meds. The worst moment was at night: there was nobody in my room, and the view of the cemetery didn't help me sleep. I was afraid of ghosts and vampires: that's why I wasn't sleeping, or maybe because I was thinking too much. And one night, with so much brooding, I had a nightmare and woke up in a sweat. I wasn't able to remember the dream, I just felt a weight in my chest and I was swallowing as if my saliva were poison. The tree branches banging against the window were tormenting me, I was afraid of the dark, and the noise of the wind only increased my anxiety. The dark blue, almost black, hue of the room allowed me, all of a sudden, to identify the root of my torment: a face. The dream was of my uncle, my mother's brother. The coldness of the room and the noisy branches made me remember an incident I had experienced against my will. I was in my maternal grandmother's house, in the hallway to be precise. Darkness dominated, punctuated by city lights that fell on the floor. I make my way to my uncle's room to sleep. That evening he has no woman with him, he is lying on his bed with an adult magazine in his hand. He looks at me and says something; I am afraid. I've always feared him. During the day he appeared calm, with that physique that many would have envied: tall, muscular, with sunken blue eyes, a straight nose and very blond hair, large hands and a serious tone of voice. At night, however, he seemed to change into an evil person. His room was filthy, the bedside table was falling over, the stereo had only one working speaker. There were candy wrappers and empty cigarette packets lying on the floor; between the bed and the wall, empty beer cans and bottles of alcohol, some broken. Only one white shirt hung in an otherwise empty, open closet. His black leather coat was resting on the chair he kept under the window. Everything inside that room stank, just like my life when I was in that house. I went over to pull the cot out from under the bed and lay down. He didn't even notice I was there, he was just lying there silently in the grip of his delirium and cigarette smoke. I fell asleep. At a certain point, I can't breathe and when I open my eyes, I see him naked on top of me. I try to scoot out from under him but he pushes me back down effortlessly. And then I scream, I shriek. But screaming is useless, so I wriggle free, gasping for air. I bite his arm as hard as I can, and I feel him stop, maybe I have hurt him. He loosens his grip for a second and I take advantage of that moment, I see my salvation. I kick him hard between the legs, he falls to the ground like a pig whose heart has burst. He doesn't even have the strength to speak and I run away. I try knocking on all the doors. My grandmother doesn't open and tells me: "Go away!" I am overwhelmed with despair. I look at my uncle's room and I think: if nobody lets me in, he will hurt me. I am exhausted, terrified. I hear him unzip something and I remember the bag he once showed me. He keeps syringes, spoons, and a knife in that bag. And I understand everything, without having to think. I hear him take this knife out, place it on the creaky bedside table, get dressed again, and say: "No one will open a door for you, I'm the only one here!" As he speaks, the cold air fills with the stench of alcohol. He appears at the door, staggering, shouting insults at my mother, howling at me: "Wretched boy!" Terror seizes my heart and I'm unable to breathe, maybe I'm unconscious but my survival instinct is intact: it is this instinct that gives me the strength to kick at the last door. He is slow, too slow to be able to escape the attention of the sensible woman behind the last door; she can't pretend she doesn't know what's happening, she has two children and is afraid for them, too, so she opens the door, lets me in and hugs me: "You don't have to be ashamed of anything, it's this place that is messed up, not this life. You are safe now." The scene grew fainter in my mind. My heartbeat was now slowing down and my chest released the weight of the anguish. I was once again perceiving the light taste of the air. I had heard those words about shame years ago but only now did I really understand them. Blaming myself for all that I had lived through, I felt a sense of shame. I was convinced that everything happened because of my existence. The words of that woman, still echoing in my mind that night in the hospital, set me free. After that moment, I began to sleep peacefully. I started sensing smells and seeing colors. I made friends with the medical technician: he was nice and smelled like lavender. So, if I had to describe that place, I would call it "the Lavender Hospital." The sense of serenity I regained also calmed the marks made by the machine on the white sheets of paper: the lines were more defined and almost all of the same color. Once again, those lines were describing my state of mind. I couldn't wait to go back to the institute to hug my sister and my friends. I spent the last three days at the hospital with Vlad, a boy with Tourette's syndrome. The first day I was afraid of him, I didn't understand his sudden outbursts and his totally random words. But then, between one twitch and another, he explained his disorder to me. It was funny, I laughed every time he spoke but he didn't take it as an offense because he understood that

I was laughing at the things he said and not at his condition. "My ass" was his most frequent refrain. "Take your medicines," they would say to him, and he would answer, "Sure! My ass! Now I *myass*take them! Sorry. My ass! My ass!," and so on and so forth.

When it was time to leave that place, I said goodbye only to Vlad and the technician. The director came to pick me up and, seeing my sullen expression on account of his "betrayal," he told me he was happy that I had found some peace again and that he wanted to treat me to an ice cream to celebrate. But, remembering how it went the last time, I retorted: "My ass!" He smiled, taken aback, but as he got in the car said, "I deserve it," and we went back to the orphanage.

~

On my return from the psychiatric hospital, I noticed spring had bloomed, even on people's faces. Everything was carefree, the light from the sky colored the kids' movements: they played at chasing the clouds and their shadows caressed the ground at every step. The attendants started organizing short afternoon outings. "Line up and be quiet!" they were always reminding us, displaying an authority that didn't really exist on those occasions. During those walks my relationships with my three friends became even stronger. Spending all our time in a room, or even in the same building, would get monotonous; there would be no new conversations, no new jokes. But, walking around, watching life flow by, we had so many things to say. Even the dreaded Ivan let the good side of his heart show. We discovered his gift for sharp observation and subtle irony. He managed to identify, in every rock, a familiar face from TV shows and he would immediately parody it. He told jokes I barely understood, but the older boys laughed and their laughter was infectious. Our walks followed easy paths: we would walk along the road and often stop among the trees. Nizhny is full of tall trees, like maples, with sturdy trunks and very large leaves that reminded me of hands. The older kids said that if a boy brought a maple leaf to a girl, made her close her eyes, and took her by the hand, she would become his fiancée if, when she opened her eyes, her hand was the same size as the leaf. But there were also birches, trees with thin white bark. They were beautiful to look at, full of tiny leaves that seemed to sing a new song whenever there was wind. One afternoon we went into the woods and stopped to watch Sergej go up to a birch tree. He was acting strangely: standing very tall with his feet hidden in a carpet of leaves, he looked like a small protuberance from the tree. He took a small knife from the pocket of his pants and started carving a hole in the bark. The attendants pretended not to see that blade; harbored in the condensation of their sighs was the hope that he would never use it to defend himself or attack others. Sergej took an empty plastic bottle out of his backpack and cut off the top. We were puzzled: our silence was like a veil that settled on the leaves and on our curious faces. From the other pocket he removed a thin string. He tied what was left of the bottle to the tree, just under the hole. He stuck a straw into the hole and exclaimed: "We'll be back in a week!" We all burst out laughing. "Yeah, sure! Laugh, all of you, laugh! Good job! I'm the only smart one here." Mild insults were thrown around but he just stood there, believing in what he had just done. "What a fool!" "Idiot!"

We had a good time at these outings. Often the person in charge of the photo lab came with us. He was a man of medium height with a prominent belly and vaguely Asian-looking eyes that squinted so much that you didn't notice his bulbous nose. He had dark skin, so we used to call him Chocolate. He promised the next time he would bring his camera with him.

The following week we went back to the tree. Ivan led the group; the woods were silent. As rays of sunlight hit the branches, they colored his face with hope. When he nodded, we reacted with screams to magnify the moment and make it more epic. And Sergej barely held back insults as we, in our rowdiness, kept hitting the back of his neck with our knuckles. Ivan continued his part in the play: he took the plastic container filled to the brim and went up to Sergej. He knelt at Sergej's feet, completely immersed in his role, and recited, raising the bottle to the sky: "Taste the drink of the gods, my son, I am not worthy. And I don't want to die. You are the one who must satisfy our thirst." By now the laughter had made our cheeks sore and filled our stomachs with air: we were full of lightness. In the throes of the performance, Sergej insulted Ivan's mother, and got ready to taste the drink himself. He turned toward us and with a mischievous smile exclaimed: "But what the fuck will you ever understand?!" After the first sip he smiled, and then his expression turned very serious and he fell to the ground. The attendants covered their mouths with their hands; we kids froze, incredulous.

We looked at one another. Mishka covered his eyes: "He poisoned himself! Now we must dig a grave here!"

Meanwhile, Sergej had jumped up to his feet again, as if nothing had happened. "You were hoping for it, huh!"

"You fool! You are a total loser."

"I wish I could die."

Ivan, once again, took over the scene, and grabbing the bottle from Sergej's hands, he poured a little liquid on the ground: "I must taste it again without the stench of his saliva." After he finished swallowing, he remained silent. He looked around for a large leaf. Then he took a deep breath. Putting the drink on the ground, he grabbed the arm of his friend, who was now a little frightened, and raised it up to the sky, exclaiming in a distorted voice: "Sergej lives on." He put the leaf on his own head as if it were a crown.

We all took turns tasting the sap, including the attendants, who were so absorbed in what was happening they drank from the same cup. And we were amazed by the sweet, good taste. The brown-haired attendant asked Sergej where he had learned to draw sap from a tree, and he, with a dark expression, retorted: "How do you think I learned?"

"Because you are a scientific luminary," someone scoffed.

"No, you idiot. We are the forgotten, the orphans."

Everything went silent, not a leaf stirred, even the wind had stopped.

"Most of you know what it feels like to die of hunger and thirst. And one night—so I didn't have to drink my own pee—I started to carve some tree bark because I remembered someone once telling me, 'You can drink a tree.' That's the whole story."

We paused for a few minutes, filled with a sense of compassion. We all knew the feeling of hunger Sergej mentioned, we had all experienced it. In that moment, I looked around for my sister, and she, too, was looking for me. Once, in desperation, Irina had started rummaging through garbage and found some packages of pasta. We ate that pasta for a week, maybe longer. It's never easy to explain the feeling of hunger that drives you to the edge, to despair. In winter, when there was nothing to eat, I would take bites of snow. Sometimes, on a lucky day, if there were snowmen around, I would steal the carrot.

The silence was interrupted by Chocolate: "Kids, I brought the camera. Mishka, stand in front of the group since you are the most handsome one!"

"Arthur, can you take a picture of us?"

"Why me?"

"Because you are the ugliest one, right?!"

It was an incredible moment, the best moment that I had ever had with them. Hierarchies and fears had dissolved: Sergej's talk that afternoon had reminded us that deep down we were all the same. The attendants arranged us according to height: I ended up in front with Sasha, Mishka, and Alyona. Chocolate set up the self-timer and, when everything was ready, he ran toward us and took his place in the last row. For the first time, the flash had immortalized us all together. When the photo was developed, you could even see the ray of sunshine that had reappeared in the trees at the exact moment of the shot, hiding Ivan's smile as he placed the devil's horns behind Arthur's head.

~

The days flew by quickly, the sun lit up the windows of the buildings with desires for freedom, highlighting the fingerprints of the kids on the glass. I was thinking about Babushka. We hadn't been able to see her since her operation. But I knew she would come to visit us soon, I craved her warmth and the smell of her small apartment fiercely.

She finally showed up one afternoon in June and was very happy to see us again. I threw my arms around her neck and in an instant her good smell made my pupils dilate and filled my heart with joy: it's a nice smell that I still carry with me. I just close my eyes and recall a moment with her: it's like recovering a sensory memory. Alyona warned me not to crush her with my embraces because she hadn't yet fully healed. But Faya reassured me: no one has ever died from hugs.

When we got to her place, she showed us her scar. On the worn-out skin of her sturdy belly there was a crooked purple line that started at the chest and ended in the area of her groin. I asked her if I could touch it and she said yes. The scar was very thick. Faya smiled: "Don't worry, it's normal for it to be tougher than the rest of my skin. Scars are hard because they allow us to become stronger." I recall these words every time I feel the weight of life on me. She was always shining and strong, and shone even brighter when she walked around the house in her robe. Her life of poverty had etched a stern expression on her face, but she was always quick to melt when Alyona and I spoke to her.

She was so happy to have us with her that she took us to a park nearby and treated us to some cotton candy. What I remember about that small park is a yellow merry-go-round that still smelled of fresh paint and a swing on which my sister played the entire time, until Babushka decided we needed to go home. There we ate some cold prepared food. She sternly reminded us to brush our teeth, and we all brushed together. I wasn't in the habit and looked stupid holding a toothbrush. I laughed watching Faya move her toothbrush up and down. Alyona brushed her teeth with her usual composure, boasting, in a mocking tone, that she was better than me. I was on the verge of kicking her but a glance from Faya was enough to quickly stop me. The three of us slept all together in one big bed.

The next day was a sunny Sunday, and we went to the market. I carried the little two-wheeled green cart with frayed and faded brown stripes, while Faya kept my other hand safe in hers. There was a strange feverishness in people's footsteps; their eyes would have bought everything, but their bags, mostly full of fruits and vegetables, were light in their hands. On the way to the market there were mostly women well into their sixties, their hair tucked in headscarves, and just a few boys and men. I had always been attracted to the smell of fish, especially the pink kind: I was hoping Babushka would buy me some. But Faya bought some beets, cabbage, carrots, half a kilo of beef, and a container of sour cream. And I was already savoring the taste of dinner: she was going to cook borscht. Before returning home, she treated us to ice cream. When we got back, she started cooking. I had been enchanted by the smell of smoked fish in the market, and I was so curious to taste it that I started devising a plan to get some. For a moment, I thought I could just go to the shop behind the building, grab some pink fish in a black package—since I was then ignorant of both the name and the taste—hide it in my jacket, and leave the shop nonchalantly. But we all know our limits: I had never stolen anything, and I was incapable of doing it without being caught. So I decided to give up on the fish idea and started snooping around the cabinets in the bedroom. Each cabinet gave off a different scent of mothballs, and I realized that even inanimate objects have their smells. I found some old faded photos in a drawer, and I recognized Faya, young and beautiful, leaning on the wheel of a big old truck. While rummaging around, a white envelope ended up in my hand. Curiosity is everything at that age, and I decided to open it. There was a hundred and fifty rubles in it, a huge amount for me, who had never held more than five rubles in my hand. An idea crossed my mind: take the money and go to the shop behind the house to buy the fish, the thing I wanted more than anything else at that moment. The idea came as quick as lightning, and I was even faster in actualizing it. I told Faya I wanted to go down to play soccer with the other kids, and she agreed after the usual dos and don'ts. I ran down nine floors, turned left, and headed for the shop. My mind was clouded by the flavor that I would taste in exchange for those banknotes I was crumpling in my palm. I stepped into the little shop, went straight to the fish section, and grabbed a two-hundred-gram black package of that pink fish. At the checkout, I impulsively decided to also buy a *sgushchjonnoe molokò*. I waited impatiently for the woman in front of me to leave. When it was my turn, the cashier, who was also the shop owner, stared at me as he totaled up the bill. He had very thick gray eyebrows, and a fishlike mouth with an expression that wavered between looking stern and bored by life. He told me the price, which I can't remember now, and I placed all three fifty-ruble bills on the counter. He left them there, kept quiet for a few seconds, and then, as his wrinkles formed a new shape on his face, asked sternly: "Where did you get that money, kid?" I turned as red as a tomato and answered with the first thing that came to mind: "I found it on the ground." He smiled and said: "Return these bills to the person you stole them from, they're not damaged, they've never been used. Give them back, and I'll treat you to some *sgushchjonnoe molokò*." Suddenly I realized what I had done: I had stolen money from a person who had always done everything for me with headaches in return. What was I doing with that money? Faya worked, and worked twice as hard when she took care of us; I was just staying in an orphanage waiting for my future, while she was, at this point, hoping for a few happy days before the end of her life. I wanted to experience the taste of pink fish with those rubles, while her survival depended on that money. I started crying in front of the cashier, who patted me gently: "I know you're hungry, we're all hungry. But don't let yourself be blinded. Fill your stomach with what you have and don't betray the trust of those who love you. You can buy back bread, but not people's trust. Look around, you see the shelves are full of food, but there is no trust on the shelves, it can't be bought or sold." He gave me the *sgushchjonnoe molokò* and walked me out of the shop, stroking the back of my neck.

I went back home and climbed the stairs with my eyes closed and full of tears; I knew those steps by heart, their number and shape. I came to our door full of shame and a deep sense of guilt. Faya let me in; she was worried after seeing me in tears. She didn't even have time to ask me anything, I just hugged her, apologizing and sobbing. She calmed me down and asked what had happened. I told her the truth; her understanding expression didn't change, though the warmth in her eyes turned to ice for an instant. Only now do I understand what her reaction was hiding: she was frightened by what I had done. She knew she wouldn't be there forever, and she was afraid of the path I might take. Perhaps the reality in which I was growing up flashed before her eyes: abandoned in an orphanage, among kids just like me, with nothing to lose. Who knew what I might do as I grew up: I could become a thief or something worse. If I hadn't gone to her voluntarily and told her everything, if, instead, someone else had dragged me home, Faya would have screamed that I should go back to the institute and hope that someone would take me into a nice house, with a cozy fireplace, someone who was able to provide the upbringing she was unable to give me. She didn't say a word about what had happened, as we enjoyed her warm borscht during dinner. Before tucking us in for the night, she said we should be happy that summer was beginning.

The next day we got up later than usual, waking up to a nice smell coming from the kitchen. Faya had prepared crêpes for breakfast; she told us to hurry up and eat because we had to be back at the institute by noon. We took the same bus as always, got off at the stop in front of the gate, said goodbye, and went back to our rooms. I kept quiet until evening, avoiding everyone because I was feeling so guilty about stealing from Faya. I thought I was a bad boy: I had betrayed the trust of the woman who was the only real hope for me and Alyona. I told Mishka the story, and he said not to worry about it: I had actually turned myself around by not taking the last step of spending that money. I was not a thief. I repeated it to myself in a low voice, turning off the light: "I'm not a thief, I will never be one." I calmed myself down and fell asleep.

The month of June flew by like the ashes of a good cigarette enjoyed in the wind: the lightheartedness burned out quickly. In the last week of June we were informed that we would spend the summer at camp. We were thrilled. But the news that we would be sent to different camps caused widespread commotion: it was possible the bonds that had formed during the cold winter would be broken. As a child, I always saw summer as an oasis in the desert. Living outdoors, in places with wooden cabins, in the middle of meadows and gardens, that's what I looked forward to all year round, and the same was also true for the other kids at the institute. Actually, for kids my age in general. Mishka, Sergej, Sasha, and I hoped right away we would end up together and imagined how camping would be for us.

During that last week, we would go up to our room after supper; through the open window the wind filled the sails of our fantasies. None of us had ever been to summer camp, so our fantasies emerged from the depths of our desires. Sergej insisted that a camp was an open space with an endless green lawn extending along a river. He imagined small blue cabins with large white windows and a few swings and bike paths marking the way to the village. Across the river, Sergej was sure there were stables with horses—all white, except for a brown one. And he would steal that horse, because he would know how to ride it and take it away; or even better, with that horse he would flee from everything and everyone, without leaving a trace. He had always said: "I'm here at the orphanage because nobody cares about me. And I don't care about anybody."

Then it was Sasha's turn. He spoke of a large forest without houses, with lots of tents and an adventurous lifestyle. He kept saying he would wear long pants because he was really afraid of snakes. He hoped there would be opportunities to get to know other children, because he already knew all the children at the institute and was not a fan of anyone else except us. Mishka and I were hoping to end up at the same campsite: more than the others, we had always imagined having this experience together. Our image of camp was based on an advertisement we had seen a few weeks earlier: THE GRASS IS GREEN, IMMERSE YOURSELVES IN THE MEADOWS, IN HOPE. A large forest, many trees with space between them, and in the empty spaces many cabins where we too would stay. With our imagination, we built a soccer field—even if neither of us was particularly athletic—and a tennis court and a dance floor. Yes, a dance floor. We swore that before the summer was over we would dance with a girl. We didn't know how, but we would succeed.

On the first of July, the destinations were announced. It was impossible, it seemed like a joke, something unreal: all four of us were randomly assigned to the same campsite. We started celebrating and throwing pillows at one another. Mishka stopped abruptly and shouted: "Now let's do somersaults on the bed; anyone who can't do them is a son of a——." Sergej, Mishka, and I laughed, those words didn't hurt us, they were sarcastic. Sasha was offended: his mother was still alive and she was a virtuous woman. His pout lasted for a few seconds. We stood at the end of each bed and at the count of three we tried doing somersaults; if things went wrong, we would only hit our backs on the mattress. Mishka and I succeeded, Sasha didn't even bother trying, while Sergej was so excited that he jumped too high, fell awkwardly on the mattress, and bounced to the floor. The laughter that followed was so out of control it made our stomachs cramp. The party was interrupted by Ivan. This time he didn't use his hands but told us to stop it immediately. We carried on giggling until it was time for dinner, where we met up with my sister and were happy to learn she had also ended up in our camp group.

After dinner, in the last flashes of light before the sun had completely set, we climbed onto the roof of the little cabin next to the institute. As the remaining rays kissed the green apples for a few minutes, Irina reappeared out of nowhere in the splendor of a summer about to begin. I had the sensation she was there somewhere, sitting on the branches of those trees, extending her arms toward me to make life serene, with that fleeting promise we both understood—a promise always ready to be quickly broken—that everything would be fine, that everything would work out. Seeing Mishka, Sergej, and Sasha next to me, I had the sensation that the sweetness of the evening was hugging all four of us.

One beautiful sunny afternoon—some days before our scheduled departure in the middle of the month—my mother's brother showed up without warning to take me out for a visit. The director was puzzled, but my uncle was persuasive; he said he wanted to take me to a merry-go-round to celebrate the beginning of summer. The director didn't notice my suspicion and fear; he was strangely distracted that day.

My uncle was wearing the white shirt that was always hanging in his closet. He was all smiles, his tone calm and kind, his gestures conveyed peacefulness: he seemed strange, unlike himself. We took a bus; I don't remember the number, but I remember that we went to a place I had never been to before. We walked down a gloomy, rundown street that ended on the bank of the Volga River. There were two benches, and my uncle told me to sit down. He sat down too. He looked confident in the sun in his well-ironed shirt and stylish pants. He was smiling, calm. He said that we were waiting for a friend of his and that the three of us would spend a nice afternoon together.

I focused on observing the flow of the river. The water was very dark and deep. I started to shiver. Soon after, his friend arrived. She was tall with wavy reddish hair and a body full of curves that looked as if they had been drawn. Uncle introduced us: "This is Kola, my unlucky little nephew. Since his mother died, I've been taking care of him." Those words left me speechless, frightened. She immediately opened up, began telling me how she too had lost her mother, how she had to run away from her abusive father. A too-familiar story in certain neighborhoods. My uncle was so into his role that he even managed to burst into tears. He was perfectly capable of hiding his evil side, she hadn't yet seen it for sure, but wickedness was probably the true essence of my uncle. She unexpectedly hugged him and said she wanted to stop thinking. And so, he assured her that they would take "the dose" and then go home. I didn't understand what the dose was.

We walked along the riverbank for about ten minutes, crossing an area full of trash and syringes, and as we wandered farther from our starting point, the air became more stagnant and the branches of the trees seemed to want to protect the sun by hiding it among the leaves. We stopped in front of a makeshift shed, assembled with scraps of all sorts: cardboard, cloth, plastic bottles, wood. Two boys were sitting inside. I like to think they were still boys so I can somehow excuse them. One was sitting on what vaguely resembled a cloth sofa; he was obese, with not much hair and a grayish beard. His nose was large and crooked, his lips were thin and barely pink. The other, seated on an old corroded tree trunk without bark, was very slim. Thick swollen veins on his bruised skin made him look like a plain teeming with rivers. He wore a pair of crooked glasses. My uncle told the girl to wait at the entrance and took me inside. As soon as they saw him, the two guys snickered. "Hey, look who's here! So, you're not dead yet! Have you brought new recruits?" asked the stocky one. My uncle half smiled, slipping into yet another role. I was afraid they might do something to me, but really, I was only there as a shield. The slim guy stared at me, his gaze then shifting toward my uncle, who didn't say a word. Next to the sofa there were pieces of wood, cans, and cigarette butts. The slim guy lost his patience: "Well, so how much do you want? One dose?" I started to get it. My uncle replied, "One," and handed him some money. It wasn't enough. The fat guy stood up, while the other one started cursing. The girl heard the shouting, went inside, sensed what was happening, took the wallet out of her purse, and handed the rest of the money to my uncle. She managed to ignore their remarks, without blinking an eye. That's when I thought of Irina: who knows how many times she had found herself in similar situations, and who knows what compromises she had to accept. I felt some relief: it's true, she was dead, but at least she wouldn't have to face situations like this one again; perhaps now, six feet under, her body was finally at peace.

We left the shed and went toward the bus stop. The farther we walked away, the more it seemed the sun wanted to leave behind its shield of leaves and embrace me. I didn't want to be there with those people. The girl asked my uncle to use the dose right away. He smiled and pushed me away with an almost threatening look: "Grown-up stuff." Stuff of despair, I wanted to yell. I couldn't stop thinking of Irina, imagining her in that situation, without any choice. As soon as my uncle took out a spoon, I started connecting the various dots. The casualness of his actions revealed that he was a drug addict, not just a pervert. When I was older, I learned that the drug he used was called Krokodil, a social plague that was taking root in Russia in those years. The user's flesh ends up falling off from the spot where the syringe enters. It's literally a flesh-eating drug. And in his case, the drug had eaten his heart at the very least. I remembered that little bag with the syringes and the knife that he kept in his room. I started feeling afraid for the girl, because I knew he intended to take her home. But what was I supposed to do? Who listens to a child? I felt guilty for my helplessness. The girl gives my uncle a kiss, his snort fills the air like that of a horse just before the start of a race. He squeezes one of her breasts and she, pleased, but perhaps also annoyed, walks away playfully. And here is my uncle, that wretched man, holding the dose, a syringe, and a spoon in his hand, unable to consider the child next to him, unable to remember that he too was once a child, unable to protect me from the possibility of becoming like him. But while the dose and the syringe are still in his hand, the girl suddenly jumps back and yells: "It's him!" In the echo of her cry, two policemen appear out of nowhere: a kick between the legs, and there he is, my uncle on his knees. In an instant he is in handcuffs.

It was all so fast that I had trouble understanding what was happening. I saw him in the police car, with bulging eyes; it seemed like his soul had been stolen: he realized that from that moment on, he would no longer be free. While the car door was still open, he motioned for me to come closer and asked the policeman for permission to take off his shirt and give it to me as a memento. The policeman said no. Then he begged to be allowed to smoke one last cigarette. This request was honored. He lit up, took a nervous puff, and started speaking to me. His tone changed: he was now docile, his eyes and nose were red, and there was a sense of relief on his face. "Kola. Nikolai Nikolajevich. You see, life comes to collect. I don't think I'm bad, but I have become bad. Like your mother, I tried one day to get up and throw away all the cans and syringes. I tried telling myself: yes, what the fuck! Fuck this shithole, now I'm going to buy myself a shirt, look for a job, and change my life. Eh, dear Kola, all the way to the store, I was determined and honest with myself. *I have to do it!* But coming back to my room, seeing it all empty, without cans, without syringes, I got scared. I was already missing the place from which I was about to escape." He took one last puff and threw the cigarette away. The girl was standing a few steps from us but looking in the opposite direction. "What the fuck!" Uncle punched his knee. "Yes, it was stupid and I knew it. But I've always been a good-for-nothing, a loser: my whole life has been filled with regrets. I didn't choose to be born in this neighborhood, I didn't choose to have an abusive father and a prostitute as a mother. I've never had a choice. Yes, it's true, I finished compulsory schooling, I believed in it. I thought I could escape, but then I gave up. You know why?" And he looked at me, waiting for a nod, to feel, at least, that he was being heard. "Why?" I stammered, holding back my tears. "Because I've never had the chance to really choose. I've always done what I saw other people do. I've never loved a woman, I've only really used women. But have you seen your grandma? She makes a living with her stinking body. I never said sorry, because this neighborhood is a war zone. And now I'm so alone and hopeless that I'm telling you, my sweet child, all my 'if onlys.'"

One of the policemen got in the car. My uncle asked again if he could give me his shirt; the policeman who was still outside gave his consent with a slight nod and took off his handcuffs. At that point, it was clear he would not try to escape. My uncle unbuttoned his shirt. "I have nothing to give you," he continued, "and you know very well that we won't see each other again. I know the harm I have caused you and your sister, but my soul is a prison. I smell the rot inside every day, and I am only capable of rotten deeds." He took his shirt off and gave it to me. "I'm not apologizing, I'm not capable. But please, keep this fucking shirt! Keep it and store it out of sight. If you ever look at it, remember that it belonged to me and that you have to do everything you can not to end up like this. Change, do it for Irina." The car door closed and from the open window, I heard a drawn-out scream that sounded like a benediction: "Do svidaniya, farewell, Kola!"

This is what I remember of his monologue, or at least the essence of what he said. I just stood there with his shirt in my hand. He seemed human for a moment, but I couldn't forget what he had done to me. One single confession couldn't wipe out the terror I felt every time I entered his room. I don't believe words can fix everything.

The policeman still outside the car approached me, stroked my face: his hand rough and icy to the point of burning my skin. And for the first time that afternoon, someone asked me: "How are you doing, kid?" I kept quiet, I wanted to yell something, but I didn't want to make the situation worse. I didn't respond to the other question either: "Did your uncle ever hurt you?" I didn't show any emotion. My head felt claustrophobic. Panic prevented me from screaming the truth as I clutched the white shirt. That white color and fabric, so pure, clean, and fragrant, made me feel sick. As the police car drove off, I was reliving the memory of a long-ago experience: my uncle was threatening to kill a neighbor with his knife because she kept me from using the bathroom. That moment and this one that I was experiencing as my uncle was taken away produced the same sensation, a bitter, hard-to-swallow taste of iron, as if my heart were pumping rusty blood to my mouth. I could still see the handcuffs around his wrists, his strong bare arms behind his back. I didn't know if I would ever see him again, I hoped not. I had also hoped for this the other time, when he had threatened the neighbor. But two weeks after that arrest he had shown up at the house, with his leather coat and those white teeth of his.

The sound of the sirens had now faded, but I was still immersed in my thoughts of all I had gone through with my uncle. I even felt pity, I tried to excuse him, to stop blaming him: in the end I surrendered to tears of exhaustion. My tears were hot, my heart was beating fast. The girlfriend, who in the meantime had kept her distance, smoking who knows how many cigarettes, took me back to the orphanage, where she informed the director of what happened. I went to my room, hid the shirt at the bottom of my backpack, skipped dinner, and went to sleep.

With that day now behind me, I never spoke of it to anyone. The departure day for going to camp finally arrived. There were many buses in front of our institute: each was heading toward a different destination. There was enthusiasm in the air, some girls cried, knowing they were going to be separated, while Alyona, my three friends, and I were carefree, already imagining what we would do at the camp. The bus was old and white with blue stripes that had almost completely faded from all the miles traversed. We sat at the back and I fell asleep.

I woke up a few hours later to the kids shouting ecstatically: we had arrived. I felt confused right away—and Sergej made fun of me—when I noted that the campsite was completely different from how we had imagined it. There was a large dirt yard with about a dozen buses, and in front of the wooden gated entrance there were at least a thousand other kids: it looked like a huge swarm of bees, voices were buzzing in rapid succession. We were in the honey of life, and we were ready to satiate ourselves and make some preserves for the years to come. The thrill of that summer, the faces of my friends and my sister: my skin never felt those sensations again; it was the summer of our lives, after months spent locked up inside the institute.

The camp counselors scrolled through the lists of children to be placed under their wings, and the lot slowly cleared. Sergej and I ended up in the same room, Mishka and Sasha in another. My sister went with the girls.

The camp had many cabins, almost all built under an age-old tree. The colors of summer entered the houses through the trees. In the evenings, when our legs finally let go of all their excitement, you could still smell the enthusiasm that would get us back on our feet the next day. There were many trails, you could skate or ride bikes and scooters; you could play any sport, and there was even an artificial pond.

We would meet for meals with the other kids in small but charming wooden structures. The mostly aqua green and brown accommodations were aging because of the light-hearted roughhousing of us kids.

One time Sergej and I argued over something trivial and stopped talking for a few hours. We skipped lunch because we didn't want to see each other. Around five o'clock in the afternoon we made up and agreed that we were both very hungry. The cafeterias were closed, so we stole a kilo of bread. The bread was kept in plastic baskets near the tables, so we opened one of them and ran off with our loot toward the pond. Between the two of us, we only consumed a third of that bread, because the entrance to our stomachs was still not used to working on large amounts of food. We used the rest to lure a black dog we had found near the pond, throwing him a few mouthfuls.

I especially remember the mornings of that very active summer. We got up around ten, because the dense branches of the trees seemed to slow down the rays of sun. We ate a quick breakfast and then decided what to do. Despite my small build, I always took the bicycle intended for the bigger kids, and I would wedge myself between the seat and the bottom part of the frame. The bigger the bikes, the more I wanted to try them. One afternoon, after lunch, the sun was beating down on the campsite, the air was thick. There was nobody on the trails. I took the bike with the largest wheels of all, wanting to take advantage of this moment when no one was using it. I went for a spin; it was a very beautiful bike, pistachio green in color, its chrome so bright it was blinding. I decided, after a while, to try going down the steepest hill. I took off my shirt, put it on my head to look like a ninja, and took a running start so I could take my feet off the pedals on the best part of the hill. And there I was, after the initial leap, ready to enjoy the speed, the freedom of the wind, with the sour taste of the gnats that, of course, ended up in my mouth. So excited by the speed, I lost my balance, the bike going to one side and my chest scraping the asphalt. I got up without fully comprehending what had happened, and I saw a stream of blood staining the right side of my chest. I didn't shed a single tear, I just went to take a shower without saying anything to anyone. But that evening I had to surrender, defeated by the burning pain. I cried when the nurse disinfected my scrapes, as she kept repeating: "That'll teach you not to hurry in life." I hated her, and I hated the bed in which I was forced to stay for some days, until the scabs fell off the infected wound and were replaced by a faint scar, which then disappeared over time.

From that moment I decided not to ride a bike anymore. I became obsessed with scooters, but even with a scooter, I had a small accident, the aftereffects of which can still be seen when I smile. I was taking a leisurely ride with Sergej when a little girl with a blond braid passed me, daring me to catch her. Here was a risk I didn't see coming: a little blond girl, still missing teeth, was challenging me. I chase her, but once again, I lose my balance and fall badly. On my teeth. I looked like a vampire, with my chin full of blood and my two small teeth on the sidewalk. That time, I screamed, and for a long time, too. I cried so much that one of the kids, who was a bully and a son of a——, called me a crybaby for several days, until Sergej beat him up for insulting me.

The days went by quickly. During the last week, sports competitions were organized, including an obstacle race. I signed up with Sasha, we were fast. While waiting in line to register, we set our eyes on some young girls as we thought of the end-of-summer dance. Sasha became obsessed with a beautiful girl with long flowing hair and he wrote her a note, to which, I believe, he never received a reply. He wrote: "I love you, do you want to dance with me?" It was his first disappointment, I presume many others followed, even though, today, I would like to imagine him alongside that girl with thick hair, because whenever he saw her, he would turn red; he would do anything just to hold her hand. At the time, the four of us had no idea how to talk to girls. I devised a plan for the very day of the dance.

The party was to start at nine in the evening in a small wooden structure to be used as a disco on this occasion. Earlier in the afternoon there would be sports competitions. So, I went to Sasha's beloved and I offered her a deal: if either Sasha or I won, she and her friend would have to dance with us. The stakes were high for Sasha, but for the girl it was a joke, sure as she was that we would never win. After all, boys older than us were also competing. So, she accepted. I came in last, and Sasha second to last: he almost cried, seeing that the possibility of meeting the girl had vanished. While all the others joked around and teased one another in the locker room, he seemed as sad as a cloudy sky that can no longer find its stars. I tried to comfort him, as I thought of a solution. Then I had an idea. I went to talk to the winner, a ten-year-old boy. I asked him if he could give his medal to Sasha for the evening, and I explained the reason. He looked at me puzzled, then started to laugh and said: "Take the medal—it's in my backpack—and return it at the end of the evening. In exchange, I'll eat your dessert tonight." I accepted, I was already planning to ask my sister to give me hers.

Sasha was thrilled to hear the news, but he started to panic: "What should I do? What do I tell her? And what if my hands start sweating?" Sergej replied, laughing: "Cover your face and everything will be fine!" Sasha was offended and ran into the room to get ready.

After supper we walked to the "disco." At the back, on the wall, there were some large speakers and an old stereo; on the ceiling, some colored lights. We waited outside, dressed for the occasion, following the advice of my sister and her friend. We wore shirts, the only ones we owned, and brown shorts. Sasha smelled good, maybe too good: he was wearing the cologne he had stolen from a boy in another room. After a while the girls arrived, and Sasha showed them the medal, as if it were an engagement ring! The girl with flowing black hair approached him, smiling. The girl who had accompanied Sasha's first love and I entered together, without talking, while Mishka was already on his honeymoon with a girl who had short brown hair.

The music took off and we started dancing, each of us on our own. No one had ever danced before, we were a disaster, but it didn't matter: we were laughing and cursing at each other, stopping only when a beautiful girl passed by. We waited impatiently for a slow song to arrive, and when it did we panicked. Two idiots! How did one dance as a couple? Then Sergej intervened. With his crude manners, he approached one of the girls, took her by the arms, and said: "Just take her hand, you bunch of faggots, reach around her back with your other hand, and sway! It's not difficult, you don't even have to talk, thank goodness!" We burst out laughing and awkwardly started to dance. I don't know which of us stepped on the girls' feet more, but aside from the beginning, the evening went as Sasha had hoped. During the slow dance, as I awkwardly held my little lady's back, I exchanged glances with Mishka, and there was a moment of complicity. A month before, we had imagined our experience of summer camp, and we had sworn to each other we would dance with a girl. We had managed to do it.

At the end of the evening, Sasha took his sweetheart back to the girls' dormitory. I didn't know her name, and Sasha never shared it. I asked him why and he said to me: "We'll be leaving soon, I don't want to connect my first love to her name, because maybe growing up there will be another, and I will link her name to the feeling of tonight; that way, I will get to marry both my first love and my forever lover." On hearing these words, the three of us old friends burst out laughing and we insulted Sasha's mother, but he was so caught up in his emotions that he didn't even get a little angry.

On the last day, something really incredible happened. Sergej had noticed a small stable of horses at the beginning of our stay. Almost everything he had imagined for our summer was accomplished. We were missing only one part: mounting a brown horse and riding away. I still remember that day, and the painting of a horse that hangs in my room today makes those memories even more pronounced. In the morning we were awakened by the screams of the camp counselors: "Sergej, where are you running to?" "Stop him!" All the kids ran down the trails to find out what was happening: there were hundreds of us all huddled together, full of curiosity. Sergej had climbed over the fence of the stable's property, and after running another hundred meters he reached the paddock. He went right up to a brown horse, managed to mount him, and started gently kicking his sides. From afar it looked like a funny scene, but it was actually quite upsetting. A neutral observer would see a boy with a backpack and a cowboy hat trying to ride a horse. But as a friend of Sergej, I saw how much he wanted to run away from his life. And at this point, Mishka started a chorus: "Sergej, run away, Sergej, fly away! Run, run like they're chasing you with a gun!" Everyone began chanting those words, and maybe the horse understood, or was just scared, because in that moment he took off.

The blazing takeoff was met with loud screams, and the more we screamed the more the horse ran, and the more Sergej understood that he was losing his grip and that riding a horse wasn't as simple as it seems in the movies. He rode about two hundred meters before falling to the ground.

"Shit! This hurts! It really hurts! My arm! My right arm!"

The camp counselors, running to him, were so worried about the pain in his arm, they couldn't find it in themselves to scold him. Once everyone calmed down and Sergej had gotten the medicine he needed and a cast, we spoke to him. He told us, dazed, excited, with adrenaline still running through his body: "The sound of the horse's hooves! I was scared but I didn't want to stop. If only I weren't such a baby, I would really be far away now. Instead, I still have to see your stupid faces!" His eyes lit up, partly because of the pain and partly because he knew that if it had depended only on him, he would have escaped: but he wasn't ready, and he was still too afraid of the world *out there*. And most of all, he was still a child, like all of us. This awareness guided us into a deep sleep for the last night in that magical place, with so much free space and so many kids. The world, the whole world, seemed contained within the confines of the camp. We were far from the noise of the city and cars. We were free from the fear of hazing, and there was so much light during the day that it made us forget we would return to the orphanage.

We said goodbye to summer as we had said goodbye to the girls on the night of the dance: "Thanks, see you soon."

~

Upon our return from vacation, at the beginning of August, the grass around the orphanage was a melancholy green, its first dark blades announcing the arrival of the new season. Nostalgic memories of summer camp blew in with the wind. The air was still warm as it entered through the building's large windows, filling the rooms with a pungent smell, the smell of dry leaves. The plants at the ends of the halls regained strength again, made joyful by the return of us rowdy kids and the sound of our carefree footsteps. School would start soon. What torture it was to think of seeing the teacher again with those little glasses and her piercing voice; how annoying it would feel to be woken up after falling asleep at our desks. Summer is every child's first love: in the middle of July it makes promises it can't keep over time, and the joy it creates dies at the sight of almost leafless trees. But just as every great love that ends leaves room for a new one, so too the summer in Nizhny assigned our carefree, throbbing hearts to the following year.

Around that time a new boy arrived, Viktor. He was eleven years old, very tall for his age, and he had so many freckles on his face that he came with the nickname Fragola Zingara, Gypsy Strawberry. We knew he was a Romani because his fame had preceded him: he had escaped from previous institutes at least seven or eight times. And when he introduced himself to us, he said: "No use in remembering my name since in a few days I'll run away from here, too." The girls' cheeks blushed when they met those small but deep eyes, he had something we didn't: the charm of a rebellious boy, the one who doesn't follow the rules. He rarely spoke, even less than me, and so he took away from me that trait, silence, which had distinguished me until then. I grew jealous of him: sometimes I wanted to be like him, have clear ideas and manage to make smart comments that would capture everyone's attention.

He was also good at defending himself, he didn't have to undergo the hazing ritual: Ivan considered him his equal despite their four-year age difference.

A fifth bed was added in our room, and he spent every night telling us his stories. He tried to convince us that he had been to America, that he had shouted in front of the Statue of Liberty: "Freedom is a fraud!" He told us that he had once been caught training a bear in a forest we had never heard of and that before the police arrived, he had enough time to share honey with the bear.

It was clear that he was fantasizing, no one believed him, but I adored his imagination. Every time he started a story about some adventure, I would close my eyes and imagine myself in his place. I felt good, I felt invincible. He never spoke about his parents, it seemed he was born all by himself. He had something extra that we didn't: grit and irony. For him, the fate that life had dealt him was not a burden.

One night, one of his stories lulled us to sleep, and the next morning his bed was empty. After only six days, Viktor had escaped. Everyone panicked; the director had a grim, worried expression, the attendants were in tears, and we kids were both happy for him and full of admiration. If only we had the courage to escape with nowhere to go.

The police brought him back three days later in the evening. From our window, we saw him defiantly sticking out his tongue at the policeman who was handing him over to the attendants. When he got to our floor we welcomed him with applause, and a girl with a high-pitched voice shouted: "Next time, take me with you." The attendants hurried us back to our rooms.

Viktor got undressed and we all noticed a long wound on his torso. Sasha asked how he got it and he replied: "I ran up against a pack of wolves."

We sent him to hell with lots of laughter and fell asleep.

~

As the first two weeks of August flew by, the sun became increasingly reserved, and the evening air was crisp.

One night I dreamed of a U.S. ten-dollar bill; it was tied to a balloon that I couldn't catch. I woke up sweating. After breakfast Alyona and I were escorted to the visiting room. We were told we would meet new people, but we didn't know who. After a few minutes of waiting, there they were, four people in the room with a fragrant fresh smell. The attendant who was there with us stood up, introduced herself to the two guests, and they introduced themselves to my sister and me. The interpreter began by explaining who those two people were. The social worker was also in the room. Alyona and I had already understood. We all sat down. I was staring at the carpet. I still hadn't looked those guests in the face. The man said something to the translator, who immediately addressed me: "Kola, don't be shy. I'm Alexsej, the translator, and these two people are Benedetto and Nicoletta." As soon as he finished pronouncing their names, I looked up. And there they were. Benedetto, a man with a bit of a belly, an autumn jacket in his hands, dark hair, a slightly protruding nose that went well with his broad face, and a red mole near his thin lips. He had a carefully groomed beard and large brown eyes that looked like two chestnuts at the height of the season. He had a fixed smile that was masking curiosity and fear. He had dark skin, olive-colored with a reddish undertone. He looked remarkably similar to my sister. My heartbeat accelerated. Alyona and I looked at each other and said a simple, shaky "Hello." Then I turned my eyes to Nicoletta. I felt a blow to my heart, as if it had stopped for a few seconds: I had already seen those blue eyes, they had already seen me. She had round, rimless glasses, red cheeks on fair skin and full lips, light hair with carefully applied highlights, and a smile that showed off perfect teeth. She was very tall. Those eyes, I couldn't manage to look at them. Where had I seen them? Where had they seen me? Nicoletta was probably having the same thought because when our eyes did meet, she wasn't able to sustain contact for long.

When they started talking, their tone was strange to me and my sister, and their language incomprehensible, but there was something warm in their words. Alexsej, the translator, was a tall and handsome young man. Later, he told us that he had studied languages in Siena. He had a quiet, measured, and confident voice. He was able to understand the couple's questions and to make them accessible to us children. He told us that they were Italians, that they were teachers, and that they had come all this way to adopt us, so that they could give us a new horizon. Nicoletta's eyes were the color of that blue sky I used to love watching so much, that sky I had to stop looking at because it made me think of Irina, of how much I missed her. But right then, I would have liked to open the window of that room, look out, and start watching the sky again. Her look resembled mine and was so reminiscent of Irina's that it felt as if she were with us there in that room. Indeed, it seemed as if Irina herself had sent those eyes to my life: I felt an immediate sense of joy to meet my mother again in a new person.

Nicoletta took a box of chocolates out of her bag and gave it to us. Alyona and I, smiling mischievously, opened it quickly, grabbed as many as we could, and tucked them away in our pockets. Three of my chocolates fell out from a hole in the right pocket of my pants. I rushed to pick them up. It must have looked funny because the interpreter couldn't keep from laughing. Then Benedetto gave me a ten-dollar bill, and I snatched it up, without hesitation, so fast I almost ripped it. I had dreamed of those ten dollars just the night before, and I was already fantasizing about what to buy and how to keep it a secret from Ivan and Arthur.

They told us how in Italy, or rather in Sicily, there was never snow, that there was sunshine every day. They spoke of a large house with a room waiting just for us. We chatted about this and that, and then Alexsej asked my sister and me if we were happy. The answer was "yes." I loosened up a bit, played with Benedetto, who tried to hug me. And when his big hands surrounded me, I wriggled out, giving him the middle finger, and everyone was surprised. For me it was normal, I was terrified of physical contact: it would be a long time before I let myself be touched. I felt like it was my fault, but I couldn't do anything about it. And all of this was clear to those present in that room that, by now, felt fantastical. Even the carpets seemed to change color, and the light coming in through the window had a new glow. Time flew by and we had to say our goodbyes. They asked me and my sister what we wanted, so they could bring it the next day. I asked for a Walkman, and Alyona asked for a teddy bear. We parted with an *arrivederci* on our lips, silent but clear and bright like the nuance of light our lives had taken on that day.

I went back to my room and, sharing the chocolates, I told my friends what had happened. Alyona did the same, and in the evening, after dinner, we talked; as always, we didn't say much, but we understood that the moment had come. I fell asleep right away, so that the night would fly by and I would see them again. The next day they brought us the gifts. I was incredulous, I was holding my first Walkman: I could spend nights listening to the old cassettes in the guest room and distract myself if ever I had a nightmare. Alyona hugged the stuffed animal as if it were her son, and between the words we exchanged and Alexsej making us laugh, we took our first photo together. I had headphones in my hand, close to my ears, Alyona was holding her teddy bear, Benedetto was smiling, the light of Nicoletta's blue eyes overpowered the camera's flash.

Nicoletta and Benedetto spoke at length with Alexsej, who explained the bureaucratic process of adoption. The two of them were supposed to leave for Italy the next day and then come back when all the documents were ready. This piece of news scared me a little: my sister and I were both hoping to leave the orphanage soon, and learning of their departure made me sad. The adults noticed it, and the interpreter reassured me, saying that everything would be just fine and they would be back soon. I gave in with a deep sigh, and when I stopped asking questions about Italy's weather, the guests got up to leave. Benedetto was holding an Italian-Russian dictionary, and after caressing me and Alyona, he tried to pronounce something in Russian, as he choked up leaving the room. It was awkward, but the meaning of the words was clear: "Ya tebya lyublyu." These words, which every child needed to hear, were now being spoken as if they expressed the biggest promise in the world: "I, Benedetto, and she, Nicoletta, we already love you. We'll be back soon." And they left the room; I took a cassette, slipped it into my Walkman, and sank into the armchair, while Alyona played with her teddy bear.

Three and a half months passed before we saw them again—more than a hundred days spent observing the large windows as they now greeted the remaining, reticent rays of sun that were preparing for their cold winter sleep. Those were days spent waiting for the two teachers, so sweet and kind, now far away. The more time passed, the more I worried about our untimely farewell. The idea that I had spent hours with strangers who had warmed my heart was now undermined by the feeling that something about me had convinced them not to return. My roommates no longer dared ask me how I was doing, my responses had discouraged them, maybe even annoyed them. Each time, one of the three asked me: "So, dumbass, how are you doing today? Will you tell us?" I replied with: "I feel like a pig that has discovered what happens in slaughterhouses, I'm waiting for something I don't even know myself."

I spent almost four months with these sad thoughts. Sometimes I convinced myself I didn't deserve happiness. I even thought that if I hadn't been born, my sister would have had a happier life and that maybe Irina, having one less burden, might have had a stroke of genius and pulled herself out of that miserable life. In those days, serenity came, like a lover, on the occasion of Faya's visit. I would have appreciated her visit more if I had realized the turn my life was about to take, if I had understood that this was the last time I would enjoy her comforting scent. It was a Thursday evening, before dinner. The late November cold gets into your bones, makes you shiver, and promises to persist for the months to come, but for me it is like an enthusiastic young boy who shows you his bedroom full of the toys he is about to play with. That same cold had kissed Faya's cheeks, turning them bright red and making her seem even more kind. She was waiting for us in the director's office, wearing a heavy khaki coat and seated in a small armchair, intently rummaging through two small yellow plastic bags. Alyona leapt on her, but I held back. Was I happy to see her? Of course I was, but I couldn't understand why she had come on a Thursday, since she couldn't take us home with her. So, I asked her. And she struggled to answer; while the soft light of the room seemed to grow dim a little at a time, her artificial serenity disappeared in small but sweet lies. She said that her work shift had changed and that she was no longer able to spend weekends with us. But the light in her eyes had already grown faint: "Did you have a good time with the two teachers who came to visit you?" She knew everything, she had come to say goodbye to us, but Alyona and I hadn't realized it yet. We wouldn't have let her leave like this, we would have convinced her to come with us. I would have dug deep into the heart of my father, who, for me at the time, was still "Teacher Benedetto." I would have dug into his life, I would have searched for a painful goodbye in his own experience, and I would have begged him to spare me that pain, especially when it came to Faya. I would have convinced them that Faya could cook for us, take care of the house while they were at school. She would tell us so much and we would learn so much from her. But in that moment, I was stupid: my focus was on what I didn't have, and I took for granted all that was familiar. The director's office took on a strange shape, the furniture seemed to age with every passing second, the plant next to the door seemed to wither and collapse, the wind stopped blowing through the windows, which now looked like two large eyes, sad and barely open; had these windows cried, the curtains too would not have been able to hold back their tears. The air became warm and all the smells became stronger; perhaps goodbyes are foreshadowed in this way. Perhaps even that room had realized that it wouldn't see Faya anymore. Babushka hugged me tightly, told me that I seemed older and that I was ready for beautiful things in life. She told Alyona to eat more, since she seemed thinner than usual. She gave us two yellow bags. Inside were some candies, a green apple, and a little toy for each of us. I got a little red car and Alyona a doll. She said something else but I can't remember what and then stood up: she didn't want to miss the bus that would take her home. She hugged me, she hugged Alyona. She was silent but smiling, and in that smile, a new light turned on. For us. With that smile she said goodbye. Sometimes, I can still feel her warmth in that light. And those hands aching from a life of daily toil, but still wise and warm, those wrinkles on her face, so sweet when she smiled, her neat but brittle hair, that nice, welcoming smell of her home, like so many old homes. I can still experience all these sensations as my own, for a few moments, before letting them go. Before their absence can hurt me again, before forgiving myself for what was unforgivable: not having told her thank you, for everything.

She made herself smile sweetly until the very last minute. Then she disappeared into the thick snow that covered the grounds of the institute, along with the shadows of the trees swaying in the wind. After dinner, the attendant told me that the next day, I would see the two Italian teachers again. I couldn't sleep that night: I couldn't wait for the hands of the clock to point to five in the afternoon the next day. In fact, right on time, as I was chatting with my roommates and looking out the window, I saw the green-petrol-colored Lada arrive. I went to get my sister in her room and we ran down the stairs, without waiting for the attendant to call us. In front of the aquarium and the open-mouthed fish looking for food among the stones, we ran into the teachers and their translator, Alexsej. Smiling—and concealing well how unused they were to the cold—they greeted us warmly: as if they had never gone back to Italy, as if we had spent those three and a half months together. The director joined us and we all went up to the visiting room. But the adults talked only among themselves and, from the look of their expressions, it must have been about serious matters. After they gave us chocolates and new clothes, the director told us half-heartedly to go up to do our homework. Before we left, Benedetto added: "Tomorrow night we will sleep all together in a hotel."

~

My last day at the orphanage started very early for me, or, rather, I didn't close my eyes the whole night before. I couldn't stop thinking about the teacher's words to me and my sister, translated by Alexsej as "Tomorrow night we will sleep all together in a hotel." While Sasha and the others were moaning in their sleep, I wondered what that sentence really meant. Now I was watching over my roommates with tenderness, as the shadowy darkness of the room hummed with their light sighs. When would I see them again? Would they also get adopted? At that point, I was sure that of the three, Mishka, a really beautiful, smart, and gifted child, would be the first to be adopted after my departure. Then it would be Sergej's turn, but they would bring him back, because he had a temper and distrusted adults. And Sasha? Who knows what would become of him. Since he had a mother, he would probably never get adopted. I watched him sleeping peacefully in the bed next to mine. He had a habit of pulling the covers over his mouth, leaving only his nose uncovered. As I watched him, I thought maybe he would finish college: I was sure he would become a doctor, because he was so calm when interacting with others. I thought maybe patients at the end of life would feel more at ease listening to his sweetly spoken words and perhaps dying wouldn't be so traumatic in the company of his reassuring presence. We never fantasized about our long-term futures. We never wondered, "What are you going to be when you grow up?," and now I understood why. We were aware, without being fully cognizant, that we were fumbling through a life of insurmountable challenges. "Let's see what happens" was the phrase that would come to mind because the life we had lived so far had deprived us of the possibility of dreaming big, of even imagining ourselves in the future. We almost never ventured outside the gate of the institute, and we never went out on our own; we had no experience of the world and what little we knew came from other kids' stories, both true and made up. We had a big TV in our study hall, but it didn't work very well, so even its stories didn't feel authentic. Of course, we enjoyed discussing the past; only the past belonged to us with certainty, even though we were slaves to the choices of others. The future, we all thought about without ever directly discussing it, was more like a dream; you know with absolute certainty that it is coming and it will bring something beautiful, but you don't know how to tell the story. We had the present: the orphanage and its rooms without horizons that became third-class tickets to the future as soon as the director first welcomed us with that sweet expression on his face. I also thought, during that same sleepless night, that we were not actually living. Does it make sense to say that a child is really alive if they don't have parents? If they don't have a home? If most of their memories are tears and scars? I don't think so. I don't think I ever felt like I was actually alive inside the walls of the institute, and I can say the same for my roommates. It wouldn't be inaccurate if, one day, I were to say: "Until I was eight, I waited and hoped, but I didn't live." Would it be a lie? I wanted to escape from that place, not because of the people, but because my life there had no direction. I feared I was in an eternal limbo without hope of ever reaching even a fork in the road: that would have already been a lot, a sign that something was moving forward. For the first time, that night, I allowed myself to think about the future.

Since I never managed to fall asleep, I decided, toward dawn, to start roaming the halls. I put Sergej's slippers on: they were more comfortable than mine, even though they were big for me. When I looked out the door, I felt something in my chest. At first, I felt a little breathless, just above my torso, but then my cheeks became hot and red: I was overwhelmed by emotion. There's no way at all for me to describe how I was feeling back then, but now, as the sunset has made its way to my desk, the shadows of all the objects around me hurl me back to that faraway morning.

On the one hand, I was really happy and especially curious to go to Italy (and dawn was, in this moment, "postmarking" this date with destiny). While on the other, I was noticing the strong attachment I felt to that hall. So, I decided to walk all the way to the end of it; no one would notice since you could only hear the noisy snoring of the night attendant. But what if he had woken up? In a matter of hours, I would be gone forever. Walking down the hall, passing one room after another, with all the doors closed, I pictured the face of every kid in the institute. Ivan first of all, who had given his imprimatur to the adoption of my sister and me as if he were the boss there. By now, I was no longer afraid of him. And then Arthur, I imagined him in bed with his little girlfriend, the two of them embracing: "Yuck!" Past the restroom, I found myself in a part of the building that I had never explored and where the girls slept. I noticed the color of the walls: they were shinier than the walls where we slept. And there were light-brown baseboards that we didn't have at all. The doors were covered with small cards and writing, and even some posters. As I continued walking, slowly, with my right arm extended and my fingertips touching the walls, I recalled the faces of all the girls in the orphanage: I would have liked to kiss each one of them. I was not sure why I felt that way, but the feeling was real. As I reached the end of the hall, I decided to stop and look out the window at the tall trees. The branches were scratching the glass of the large window and looked like they wanted to say goodbye. Those trees had once been the scene of a battle between our orphanage and another institute, for deaf kids. I laughed out loud, remembering how Yuri, one of the rowdier kids in our group, threw a stone at one of the kids who had attacked us: it hit him in the chest and Yuri was bragging as if he had won an important trophy but he got so distracted by his excitement that he, too, got hit by a rock and he dropped to the ground as if dead. Everybody laughed that afternoon; we were worried, but at the same time, there was a feeling in the air that our fight was not really dangerous, just childish behavior. I was lost in those memories, when I felt a hand touch my shoulder. I was startled, but it was just Mishka, still half asleep: "What the hell are you doing? Go back to bed!"

"What do you want from me? Why don't you go to bed?" I retorted peevishly, but I was also happy not to be alone anymore in the hall.

"I got up to go to the bathroom, I saw that your bed was empty, and I woke up all the others, but nobody knew where the heck you were."

"Goddammit, stop worrying about me. I've already been adopted and all of you are still orphans," I said with a smile.

Mishka punched me and told me to go get dressed.

Right then I didn't get what he meant, but later, it became clear they all wanted to spend our last hours together. So we got dressed and went outside. We decided to pick apples on the grounds next to the institute and eat them on the roof of the cabin for the last time. We had never been outside this early: it was freezing, and Sergej muttered insulting remarks that were hard to understand. In the silence of the morning, we could hear the snow creaking with every step, like an old gate driven by the wind. This sound accentuated the absolute silence; the only other sound we could hear was our chattering teeth.

"C'mon, let's go back to sleep, goddammit," Sergej kept repeating.

And Mishka responded: "Stop being such a pain! Just hurry up and jump over the fence and pick four apples."

"But why do *I* have to do it?"

And so, I replied: "Because if they catch us, you are the fastest and, besides, have you looked at your face? You look like a moron, you can say you were sleepwalking."

"*You're* the idiot, Kola. The only reason I'm not beating you up is that I want them to take you to Italy."

"Stop babbling, you bed-wetter. And move it, we're freezing."

The others laughed; Sergej was pissed, but he decided to use that energy to jump over the fence. He picked four apples: three red and one green. He handed me the green one, still complaining: "Here, idiot! It's a good thing you're leaving. Now we can sleep in peace!"

Mishka replied rudely: "You've been sleeping your whole life. You know what they say?"

"What?"

"The early bird catches more fish!"

"Who cares? The Volga River is frozen anyway!"

We all burst out laughing, climbing up to the roof of the cabin.

That was the last dawn I saw in the company of my first real friends. We sat on top of the hut, eating our apples, so cold that our teeth ached. Between the beauty of the dawn and the awareness of our imminent farewell, we weren't able to utter a word. Sasha was the calmest one, biting his apple and playing with the morning mist: "I am smoking and munching at the same time. I am *smonching*."

We burst out laughing again, but our laughter was interrupted by a loud shout: "What are you doing up there? Get down immediately!"

We got scared because we realized it was the director. It was unusual to hear him shouting. As I climbed down from the roof of the cabin, I said my last farewell to that view: a view of the apple trees—either bare or full of fruit—and the irregular little road barely visible in the distance through which I tried to reconnect with Irina. It felt like the sun was smiling at me as I slid from the roof for the last time. The director wanted to keep scolding us but realized the reason for our outing; Alyona and I were leaving the orphanage later that day. He turned around, without saying a word.

We went back to our room. Nobody spoke. Sergej went back to sleep. Sasha was staring at the ceiling, and Mishka stood at the window with me looking out at the grounds covered with snow.

We were silent until lunchtime, the last lunch for my sister and me. The director decided to eat with us and gave a speech, which I still remember well: "Kids, today is our last lunch with Alyona and Kola! Don't be sad if they have attained all of your desires or if the two teachers embody the goodness of humanity. Starting tonight, they will stay with their new parents or, better still, with *their* parents. Should they be scared? Yes, of course. I, too, am afraid but how can one be afraid of goodheartedness, or of the thirst for love of two teachers who have come from so far away? No. For them, this is no time to be scared; they no longer have to feel cold in the night or wonder what will happen next. For Kola and Alyona, it's time to think about what will happen in one, two, three, or ten years. You know that I have often spoken of this place as a garden, in which you are the fruits and flowers. Kola and Alyona are now two ripe apples that are about to be picked. Life is so beautiful today! Today is a day of celebration, and I want you to eat and enjoy this lunch of chicken and potatoes donated by Kola and Alyona's parents. Let's give it up for them!"

Everybody started applauding, shouting, and laughing. It was an incredible commotion at the tables, and no one stepped in to restore order. It was a wild celebration of life and its transformations. I was moved but didn't cry just yet. I didn't even eat, I just set aside that last green apple for later. Once back in the room, I decided it was time to gather my few belongings and fill my backpack with the new sweater the teachers had given me the night before, a pair of pants, and the little red toy car. The other kids had gone downstairs, some were in the workshops, some went to study, and I was in the room by myself. The sun was shining on the snow. For the last time, I placed the apple on the windowsill and looked out in the company of Irina. As I was looking at the apple, I remembered the day Babushka pointed out different kinds of apples to me. That afternoon, at her place, on her large bed, I was playing with my toy car, and the green apple was there next to me. She asked why I had this odd habit of just keeping it there to admire and not eat. I explained the reason and she, a little choked up, told me the name of the apple variety with that color was Simirenko.

"If one day you want to buy one, you will know which one to ask for," she added with a motherly tone, as if she wanted to reassure me that I would always be able to find my mother, in some way.

Then my thoughts turned to Irina. I wanted to feel her closer, but now, she felt very far away. My heart was beating crazy fast, I realized it was really happening: in just a few hours my life was really going to change. I was about to start living, to stop waiting, to let go of my night fears forever. Who knows what Irina might have said? Children tend to see only the good side of things and I was like that too, when I still lived with her, but right now, terrible memories were also appearing in my mind. I always wanted to blame fate and never blame my mother. In that moment, it was as if I had to choose a way to say goodbye to that room and to my apple ritual.

But how is that possible? Two people who don't know me or Alyona decided to travel who knows how far to come and get us, and you, who were just a few steps away, didn't do anything. And yes, okay, you did not have a job, and, I get it, drinking made you feel better, or at least that's what you thought, and I even get it that every man promised you who knows what before throwing you away like a boring toy. But didn't your love for us ever move you? I don't know where Italy is, I don't even know how many meters there are in a kilometer, but I know for certain that these two teachers have traveled so many kilometers from very far away to give their love to two children for whom they are not responsible. And you? You were responsible for us! You didn't love me and Alyona enough! Maybe it's love that moves everything! How would I know? I don't know, but I feel it is this way. I know Babushka did everything she could for me and my sister. I remember the nurse Katiusha, who, in order to make me keep my promise, stopped smoking as soon as I left the hospital. Mishka and Sergej defended me, and the director treated me affectionately. And these are all people who have nothing to do with me. You were, for me and Alyona, our only blood relative. You should have done everything for us! And you know what? I'm telling you that blood relationships don't count for anything, and I'm not saying this just about you. If you could only see how many desperate children live in this building. Where are their relatives? For the most part, they are abandoned children like me and Alyona. Yes, abandoned. Because we were living in an orphanage, while you were still alive. And it's not as if you were worried about finding a better solution for us. Babushka had to take care of that, holding our hands tightly and pulling us through the streets in the cold. You hadn't even noticed our situation. No, no more talk of these blood connections. "Love moves everything." If you want to know what I mean by those words, I mean the difference between giving birth to a child and taking care of it. To be born takes one day, to live takes years! And now, as I talk to you, I am crying. Because all my life, I have defended and excused you, but I only did it because I hadn't yet met anyone who could take care of me and my sister. I was desperate, lost, scared. And I took refuge in you, in those brief happy moments with you, and didn't think about all the times we didn't matter to you, like when you used to take us with you to your clients, leaving us in another room in the house to hear your screams, and we just had to sit there with our hearts in our throats from the fear. And you never considered any of this a problem. And now that I am leaving, I am angry. I would like to bring you here, even just for a day. So that you understand what you missed, so you understand that no bottle—oh, if only you had seriously tried—can fill your heart like a grateful child, and it wouldn't have mattered if you had given me only one coin or just one embrace, I would have known that you were doing the best you could! And if you—and not someone else—had been the one to take us to the orphanage and to reassure us before leaving. . . . And what tortures me the most is the fact that being separated from us probably made you plunge into the ultimate darkness. But am I allowed, as a child, to have thoughts like these? And didn't you, as a mother, worry about us? I always tried to understand you, but now you are dissolving in my heart. No, I can't do this. It's not your fault, it's not mine. Maybe it's nobody's fault. "Things went the way they went" is a nice expression adults use, but they have already lived their lives and they know what it means to accept the past, while as a kid, I didn't know yet, and I am only getting it now. I can't explain this heavy feeling, but it hurts: it's as if a sigh, bitter from life's experiences, entered the throat, and the pain removed the oxygen, leaving only bad air to damage the heart. And you feel the pain in your chest, but it's only a symptom: the illness, that is your absence, is incurable. Do you get what I'm saying? I am angry. Maybe I am being harsh, even too harsh. But I am also just a child, and my days have never been happy. I have always carried a burden that sometimes felt like guilt, other times like shame, and still other times like self-erasure.

I could have left that room and that apple on the window, carrying all my rage with me, but I decided not to. It gave me some relief to unburden my heart, it was like mourning a loss or separation.

So, I stopped thinking. I stared at the apple and its reflection in the window. And now, in my mind's eye, I was seeing Irina for the last time in her most elegant dress, as she opened a familiar door, that very same door of the orphanage through which I saw her leaving me behind. Now, in my reverie, I see her opening it again. She is smiling, with pink lipstick enhancing the whiteness of her teeth, and there are no purple marks under her eyes. Her curly, fragrant hair swings with every small step she takes toward me. She is holding a transparent bag full of apples in her hand. Green apples, five green apples and a rotten one, just like when I saw her for the last time. She comes close and gives me a kiss on the forehead. Without a word, she takes the rotten apple from the bag. She puts it in my hand. She lowers her eyes, then looks up at me. "I have to go. You do, too. I stopped by to say goodbye and give you this apple. I will keep the other five, so that I can talk to you. Right now you just need one, to start your new life. For me there will never be enough, I will always want to talk to you. We will always know how to find each other." And she opens that door again, which now looks out to a huge apple orchard, and before leaving, she turns to me one more time. She is smiling. My eyes gently rest on the apple she has just given me. It is no longer rotten, it no longer smells rotten: it is green. "It's so beautiful, Mom, to see you smile."

"It's so beautiful to see who smile? . . ." I was interrupted by the voice of Mishka, who was now sitting on his bed. I looked around, I had imagined everything. But I was not disappointed, I was happy to have had, after so many years, a meeting with Irina, even an imaginary one. This is how I said goodbye to her.

Then from the window I saw the green Lada arrive.

The time had come.

The director joined us in the room. Most likely he had been observing me outside the door. "Why are your eyes red, Kola?" he asked. "Especially now that you are leaving?"

"Yes, especially now."

"Stop it, or Mishka will start crying, too."

"That's not true. I never cry," he answered, unsure.

"I don't care if he cries too. Anyway, he wouldn't understand the reason."

"And you, Kola, do you understand the reason for your teary eyes? Would you like to tell me?"

"Well, I . . . I'm not sure, I got angry at Irina, but I don't think it's fair, and afterward, I imagined her in a happy moment."

"It's normal to be angry sometimes, Kola."

"For no reason?"

"Yes, for no reason. Or rather, without a specific reason. Maybe, there are reasons that accumulate over time, and, sooner or later, that anguish will have to come out somehow. What do you think? Otherwise, we risk going crazy."

"So, I am not a bad person if I was angry at her for a bit?"

"No, of course not," he smiled.

He took the chair from under the little desk in the middle of the room and sat next to me, while Mishka was looking at us in absolute silence; he was listening, like he wanted to learn something, or maybe, he was just sorry and didn't know what to say.

"We always get angry with the people we love. Especially when some things do not go the way we hope."

"I think my only fear is that I will forget her."

"Ah, Nikolai Nikolajevich, I understand now! It's good that you cried. Those were the tears of a man."

"I'm afraid I will forget her."

"No, Kola, don't talk like that. Just now you are upset, because you are about to experience a big change. Don't be afraid: you will not forget her. And you should not be angry at her. What will change if you cry and stay angry?"

"I don't know. I never know a fucking thing."

The director's expression changed, he understood that I was really worked up. He knew that I didn't usually use bad language in front of adults. He stood up next to me, his eyes looking toward the garden. Mishka did the same, resting his lips on the glass so that you could see the vapor from his breath.

"Sometimes life is like this, and we grow by moving on."

"Then I can't wait to be a grown-up."

"Let me share a big secret with you: the first step in becoming an adult is accepting what happens and forgiving the people who hurt us."

"Then I need to forgive Irina right away! But how does forgiveness work? Besides, I have always forgiven her."

The director smiled once again and he stroked my hair: "Well, from the little I know, forgiving those we love is not that difficult. In fact, the more you love a person, the easier it is to forgive them. And you forgive when you stop blaming them for what they did to hurt you."

The sound of a harmonica was coming from next door; it must have been Sergej, who took the opportunity to play while Ivan and Arthur weren't there. It was his way of saying goodbye to me. Mishka and I laughed, thinking of how he used to be so bad at playing the harmonica and how he had promised that one day he would learn. And now he was so good at it.

"Irina is forgiven forever, as always! So, it's life that is to blame!"

"Kola, sometimes, there is no blame!" Mishka cut in.

Now I was staring at him as if his words annoyed me, but in fact, I had forgotten he was in the room.

The director sighed, saying: "Okay, so we blame chance, we blame life. But life is actually asking for your forgiveness, by giving you a second chance. And don't be angry at Irina, she wasn't able to be there. So many are unable. And you will understand when you grow up. Don't think about all the negatives. Remember how, during these two years, you met Sasha, Mishka, and Sergej. And you met me, too!"

He was persuasive and we were quiet for a few seconds, and then the director walked out without saying any more, closing the door behind him.

I picked up the apple, and Mishka came closer.

"Are you really leaving?"

"Yes," I replied while playing with the apple, but no longer near the window.

"You are such an asshole! This morning I got so scared when I didn't see you in the room."

"Why?"

"Because I thought you might leave without saying goodbye; you're so distracted!"

"What are you, a faggot?" I reacted, laughing.

"No, you are my friend."

I was quiet once again; I was not expecting such warmth in his words. Nobody had ever called me "friend"; I mean, yes, I spent a lot of time with those kids, but that word had an effect on me. I had no idea who I was or where I was really going once I left the orphanage. And hearing someone call me "friend" gave me confidence. If somebody had asked me right then, "Who are you?," I could have said, "I am Kola, a friend."

Mishka broke the silence again: "And we will miss you, you idiot. I don't know why, but with you, there was balance in our small group."

"I will miss you, too."

"Will we always be friends?"

"Well, of course, goddammit! What does it matter where we are?! You were, and you will always be, my first friend. Every time I think of the word 'friend,' you will come to mind."

We tried to laugh, but before I left he told me one last thing: "Leave the apple on your bed, and we will keep it there until another boy takes your spot. So, in a way, you will stay with us for a while."

"C'mon, apples don't really talk, right?"

"No, but they listen." And I realized that he was referring to me and to my "ritual" with Irina. "Listen, Kola, I am not going to go down to say goodbye, I can't handle it. Let's say goodbye now, with a handshake." And then, right as we shook hands: "Faggot!" Pause. "Do svidaniya."

I was the one to leave the room first, hastily gathering all my things. And I went away quickly. I was crying like crazy. Going down those stairs for the last time, I smelled the aromas coming from the kitchen. And passing by the entrance to the dining room, I saw the two cooks with their cigarettes in hand. I didn't say anything, and neither did they. They were smiling, as I went off.

Once downstairs, I greeted the two teachers coldly, but they understood and said nothing. Nicoletta was wearing a dark brown jacket with a fur collar, and she happily displayed her smile and her really white teeth. Benedetto was wearing a black hat, a dark blue jacket, and large black boots. They were friendly, happy, their blushing cheeks betraying their emotions. Alexsej was also there. He told me that I could say goodbye to whomever I wanted, that there was no hurry. All the while, the social worker remained aloof, observing the indifferent fish in the aquarium.

So, I went straight to the woodshop to say goodbye to the carpenter: he was the first to teach me something. I hugged him in tears and promised that I would never forget him. His glasses fogged up and he said: "Go, Kola, go!"

Before going back to the hall, I bumped into Ivan near the aquarium. I was afraid, but not too afraid. I didn't know what to tell him.

"You lucky guy! If you ever come back here again, I will beat the crap out of you! You are incredibly fortunate. Now, leave before I punch you in the mouth!" I smiled and ran away.

Then I said goodbye to the director, who, for the first time ever, wasn't smiling. Choking up, all he said was "Ciao, Nikolai Nikolajevich." I hesitated, I would have liked to add something, to thank him. But, as we all know, gratitude is difficult to express, especially for those who are afraid of emotions. I hugged him quickly and said: "Let's go, before I change my mind." And everyone smiled, thinking that in some way I had finally accepted the idea that this time, fate depended on me alone. We got into the car, and all the kids were looking out from their windows, but there was nobody at the window of my former room. I felt hurt. The sky was nearing sunset, a little blue, a little bright orange. Alyona was calm, I was crying.

As the car was taking off, I turned around to see Sasha, Sergej, and Mishka running behind us, screaming: "Write when you get to Italy! Write, even if you don't know how!"

Those were the only words I caught: it was Sasha's farewell.

I hadn't said goodbye to Sergej and Sasha, because I knew they wanted to avoid the farewell. They weren't ready, nobody was. And maybe, no one ever is really ready. The car, with the social worker at the wheel, passed through the gate in a few seconds; now, you could only see a shadow of the institute and that shadow grew smaller and smaller, until it disappeared.

These people sitting next to Alyona and me couldn't have been more remote from our past and yet, at the same time, they were our future. They came from who knows what kind of experiences, they spoke another language. Alyona and I knew that this encounter with them was the first step toward new possibilities. It was as if present and future were now walking at the same pace, as if they had signed an agreement to pull the plug on the past, irreversibly. From now on, our present life could only be projected toward the window of the future. Every emotion, every fear, every uncertainty that was burrowing into our chests with each passing kilometer of the drive dissolved as soon as our eyes met those of the two teachers, our new parents. It was an odd feeling: we trusted them but, at the same time, we were afraid. Oh, adults. Who could ever really understand them? What is it that allows a child to intuit that a person will not harm them: a smile, a caress, a candy? I was deceived several times. I had to find a rationale to let myself trust, and I had to do it fast, because Alexsej would say goodbye once we got to the hotel. I didn't know how to find an answer, and even today, I still don't know. But I think that in that difficult situation, trust was automatically released from the sum of small things adding up. Alexsej kept observing me and may have understood my emotional state, because he was smiling at me. My eyes moved from that smile, which made me blush, to the two teachers; Nicoletta was holding Alyona in her arms. The two teachers were talking to each other; they loved each other. I couldn't understand them, but I didn't ask Alexsej to translate, it didn't matter to me what they were saying. I was focusing on their expressions: their wide happy eyes, relaxed mouths, and imperceptible breathing. From time to time, Benedetto would say something to Alexsej, who answered absentmindedly: most likely he didn't want to break up the complicity between the two teachers in the peace of that car. I examined their clean hands, with just a few wrinkles and no spots. Their teeth were incredibly white and their hair neat and fragrant. They smelled nice, in general, and wore new clothes without tears or patching. And most importantly, their words didn't smell of alcohol, so they were true, authentic. They were all that Alyona and I had almost never experienced in two adults who were supposed to take care of us. And besides all of that, they held hands: no man had ever wanted to hold Irina's hand. These two really loved each other, I thought. Trust was among the six of us riding in that old green Lada. So strange, I kept thinking, with a smile: for eight years I have lived in much larger spaces and the only place I ever found trust was in the sweet expression of Babushka.

We arrived at the hotel.

The social worker left us abruptly, as she had to go back to the office to take care of one last business matter. I felt nothing as I said goodbye: for her, we were just paperwork, and maybe, detachment was necessary in her job.

There were five of us for a few more minutes. Then, Alexsej warmly said goodbye to our parents. You could feel so much emotion in the air: for Nicoletta and Benedetto, he had probably been like the obstetrician who introduces expectant parents to their child for the first time, looking at a sonogram together. Words had been sufficient in our case: their innocence, their hope, their power. Afterward, Alexsej said goodbye to Alyona and, then, to me.

Up until that moment, I had hoped that he would come with us to Italy: he seemed like a very special person. His calm manner, his confidence in translating, and his warm voice made him extremely pleasant to be around. He told me to be good, not to be too hyper, and to always listen to Nicoletta and Benedetto. I hugged him, saying: "I promise." And I said goodbye, asking him: "And you, do you promise you will come and see us in Italy?"

He walked away, smiling like someone who would have loved to come visit us but, knowing he had to reckon with his own life, could say nothing.

In the five days that preceded our departure, Mamma and Papà tried every possible way to make themselves understood. Sometimes it was incredibly difficult, weird, and funny all at the same time. In restaurants, I got into the habit of ordering everything on the menu: I would taste all the dishes without finishing any of them. Benedetto would take care of cleaning off the plates. The days went by quickly and happily in Nizhny. We went to Moscow by an overnight train. Trains have always fascinated me. But what really struck me then, for the first time, was the sound of the tracks: it was relaxing for me in a special way. That constant sound filled my mind, so I didn't have to think. And I liked that.

In Moscow, Mamma and Papà took care of the remaining paperwork until the day of departure arrived. At the airport, the thermometer under an advertising billboard read −38 degrees Celsius: it seemed about right, Russia was always cold for me and Alyona. Both in winter and in the summer.

On the plane, Papà tried to teach us a card game, Seven and a Half, which we played with Sicilian playing cards, but I wasn't very into it. During the flight of about four hours I was lost in my thoughts. An airplane is different from a train. It is faster and yet it feels stationary and less noisy. I was thinking of Babushka, for me, the most important person, the one who had laid the foundation for my future. I would have loved to hug her again, one last time. Just one last moment with her warmth and her smell. The same candies, if you could find them in the supermarket, had a different taste when they came from her hand. "Of course, she worked in a train station," the words burst out of me all of a sudden. And now it was clear to me why I was so calm on the train from Nizhny to Moscow. It was as if she had been the one guiding us along the tracks, toward our future. She had kept us company that last night. Thinking this was nice and made me feel good. But it would have only been right to tell her, "Thank you"—the most important words—one last time. Thinking of her made me lose all sense of time. We landed in Rome. It was almost noon. The light coming through the windows of the plane was hot, as if the sunrays had collided with a diamond. Mamma and Papà tried to explain to us what we were going to do in that city. And since it was the 6th of December, which is Saint Nicholas's Day, they asked me what I wanted as a gift. I didn't understand the purpose of that holiday, and even less the reason for a gift, but I didn't wait to be asked twice: I requested a bicycle. We waited for other people to get off the plane first, so that we could get our hand luggage with no pressure. I heard people speaking an incomprehensible language. I told Alyona with cockiness:

"Ah, these people speak English. Don't worry, we will learn it soon."

"We're in Italy, you idiot."

I started laughing, and soon, it was our turn. I felt a sharp pain in my chest, like a one-ton ball of lead. It was a crushing sensation, a heavy weight. I took out my backpack and, opening it instinctively, emptied it in a rush to find my uncle's white shirt at the bottom. I had put it there the evening of his arrest and then completely forgot it. I heard his words again and did not want to hear them, but they were there in my head. I realized that I had left the most important people in Russia, and as I was thinking, all that went through my head were the smiles of Irina, Sasha, Sergej, Babushka, Mishka, the director, Aleksej, and even the nurse. All these people had been good to me and I had seen them all smile. But my uncle had not been good to me, and he had never smiled at me. This thought was haunting me, as Mamma, Papà, and Alyona were already on the stairs, disembarking from the plane. I didn't want to step on Italian soil for the first time, in my new life, with the thought of somebody who had hurt me. So, while Papà was yelling to me, "Hurry up, Nikolai, otherwise you'll go back to Russia!," I looked at that shirt for the last time and, without any pity or compassion, but only the desire to break free, I left it on the middle seat. Now that I am about to finish smoking my umpteenth cigarette, while around me, the room has grown dark, except for the lamp; now that the cypress tree in front of the window is a moonlit shadow and the drawing of the horse is hiding behind the curtain no longer stirred by the wind, I relive the words that had thus far marked my life in Russia in a negative sense, but that I managed to utter one last time, changing their meaning.

After leaving the shirt behind, I went down the stairs and joined my father; he took my hand, and I looked at the plane one last time: “Do svidaniya, farewell.”

~

What is courage?
It's not leaving a woman
alone to manage her two children
in the Russian winter.

It's trying not to abandon yourself
when a man abandons you
and you have two children.

It's not fearing loneliness
as you let go of a niece and a nephew:
you have loved them like your own children,
you took them to work
you fed them by sharing the little you had
you took them to the market
you cared for them at night,
you saved them by letting them go
away from the cold of Nizhny.

It's taking in two children,
whose hearts are in part
resting under the light snow:
loving them as if they had always been yours.

Courage is never forgetting,
carrying yourself along everywhere.
Revealing yourself to those who love you
because they know how to remain silent.

Just this.
And you will always be loved.

Author's Acknowledgments

Writing about one's life is like sitting on a swing: one moment you experience the highest point with lightness, the next you are afraid of falling. Behind the swing, different people stand to push you and provide stability, as in the production of a book. It all depends on them. This is why I want to thank Chiara Valerio, who continues to believe in my writing; Carola Susani, who is a mentor and close friend to me; and all the people who work behind the scenes at the Italian publisher Marsilio.

For the translation, an immense and profound *grazie* goes to Teresa Fiore, who with time has become a friend of mine. She has strongly believed in this book and the possibility of translating it, allowing me to discover meanings that I had not captured ever before (they say it often happens to authors with the translation of their books, and this comforts me). Thanks again to Daniela Chaudhary Fiore, who has filled this book with meaning, adding an infinite value to adoption and the constant search for oneself.

I am indebted to Alessandro Vettori, Eilis Kierans, and Sandra Waters of the Other Voices of Italy series, as well as the entire team at Rutgers University Press. Special thanks to Loredana Polezzi.

May the reading of this book always stay with its readers, the same way the memory of Patricia Chendi will stay with me. She was a fundamentally important person in the production of my first novel, but most of all in the publishing sector in Italy.

To my family, all of it.

Notes on Contributors

Nikolai Prestia was born in 1990 in Nizhny Novgorod, Russia. At the age of eight, together with his sister, he was adopted by an Italian couple living in Sicily. He earned a law degree from the University of Siena and currently lives in Rome. A largely autobiographical work of fiction, his first book, *Dasvidania* (now *Farewell to Russia: Memories of When I Was Kola*), was published in 2021 and included in the Universale Economica Feltrinelli series in 2024. In 2022 it won the Massarosa Literary Prize for Debut Novel, was long-listed for the Comisso Prize, and was short-listed for the Zocca Giovani Prize. His second novel is titled *La coscienza delle piante* and won the 2025 Comisso Prize (Under 35 category). He is currently writing a sequel to *Dasvidania*.

Teresa Fiore is the Inserra Endowed Chair in Italian and Italian American Studies at Montclair State University in New Jersey. The recipient of several fellowships (De Bosis, Rockefeller, Fulbright), she has held visiting positions at Harvard,

Yale, New York University, and Rutgers University. A widely published scholar of migration studies, transnational literature, and postcolonialism, she entered the world of adoption studies as a teacher and researcher after becoming an adoptive mother (in Spanish) and translation studies as a coordinator of public talks, workshops, and student internships on campus. Fiore is the author of the pluri-awarded book *Pre-Occupied Spaces: Remapping Italy's Transnational Migrations and Colonial Legacies* and numerous articles in Italian, English, and Spanish about twentieth- and twenty-first-century Italian literature, theater, music, and cinema. She has cotranslated a collection of experimental poems edited by Renato Barilli and an essay by Sherry Simon about German de Staël and Gayatri Spivak for a volume on women and translation. Her current research projects are "*Memoria presente*: The Common Spanish Legacy in Italian and Latin American Cultures," partially supported by the National Endowment for the Humanities; "Food, Migration, and the American Myth in Sicily at the Time of the WWII Allied Landing"; and "Adoption Studies." Since 2011, she has directed a program of interdisciplinary events about Italian culture in a transnational perspective (montclair.edu/inserra-chair).

DANIELA CHAUDHARY FIORE attended LaGuardia High School (Fine Arts Department) in New York City. An older adoptee from Colombia to the United States, she is trilingual: her first mother tongue is Spanish, her second mother tongue is Italian, and the language she adopted is English.

Loredana Polezzi is the Alfonse M. D'Amato Chair in Italian and Italian American Studies in the Department of Languages and Cultural Studies, Stony Brook University, New York, and an honorary professor of translation studies in the School of Modern Languages, Cardiff University, Wales, United Kingdom. She previously held positions at the University of Cardiff and the University of Warwick, United Kingdom. She is a fellow of the Learned Society of Wales and a previous president of the International Association for Translation and Intercultural Studies. Her research interests combine translation and transnational Italian studies. She has written on travel writing, colonial and postcolonial literature, translingualism, and migration. Her current work focuses on memory, mobility, and translation in transatlantic Italian cultures. She is coeditor of *The Translator* and of the book series Transnational Modern Languages. Her recent publications include (also as coeditor) *The Routledge Handbook of Translation and Migration*, the special issue of *Forum Italicum* "Critical Issues in Transnational Italian Studies" (57:2), and the volumes *Creatività Diasporiche. Conversazioni transnazionali tra teoria e arti*, *Transcultural Italies: Mobility, Memory and Translation*, and *Transnational Italian Studies.*

Titles in the **Other Voices of Italy** series:

Carmine Abate, *The Round Dance*. Translated by Michelangelo La Luna

Giuseppe Berto, *Glory: The Gospel of Judas, A Novel*. Translated by Gregory Conti

Giuseppe Berto, *Oh, Serafina!* Translated by Gregory Conti

Adrián Bravi, *My Language Is a Jealous Lover*. Translated by Victoria Offredi Poletto and Giovanna Bellesia Contuzzi

Angelo Cannavacciuolo, *When Things Happen*. Translated by Gregory Pell

Shirin Ramzanali Fazel, *Islam and Me: Narrating a Diaspora*. Edited by Simone Brioni. Translated by Shirin Ramzanali Fazel and Simone Brioni

Anna Maria Gehnyei, *The Black Body*. Translated by Eilis Kierans and Sandra Waters

Alessandro Giardino, *The Caravaggio Syndrome*. Translated by Joyce Myerson and Alessandro Giardino

Ugo Boncompagni Ludovisi, *The Twilight of Rome's Papal Nobility: The Life of Agnese Borghese Boncompagni Ludovisi*. Translated by Carol Cofone

Geneviève Makaping, *Reversing the Gaze: What If the Other Were You?* Translated by Giovanna Bellesia Contuzzi and Victoria Offredi Poletto

Dacia Maraini, *In Praise of Disobedience: Clare of Assisi*. Translated by Jane Tylus

Dacia Maraini, *Life, Brazen and Garish: A Tale of Three Women*. Translated by Elvira Di Fabio

Porpora Marcasciano, *AntoloGaia: Queering the Seventies, A Radical Trans Memoir*. Translated by Francesco Pascuzzi and Sandra Waters

Luigi Pirandello, *The Outcast*. Translated by Bradford A. Masoni

Nikolai Prestia, *Farewell to Russia: Memories of When I Was Kola*. Translated by Teresa Fiore and Daniela Chaudhary Fiore